Jack and the Time Machine

JACK

—— and the ——

TIME MACHINE

SCOTT JONES

Hermitage Press

hermitagepress.org

First published in Great Britain in 2023 by Hermitage Press Limited, Cornwall hermitagepress.org

Printed and bound in Britain by TJ Books Padstow, Cornwall

A CIP catalogue record for this book is available from the British Library.

Cover design and illustrations: Lucy Smith

ISBN: 9781739856878 (paperback edition)

ISBN: 9781739856885 (electronic edition)

In loving memory of
Jean and Herbert Mitchell.

2012

PROLOGUE

Jack Mitchell wasn't like other 11-year-old boys. Well, not in the usual sense. It's not like he had seven fingers, or three heads. No, nothing like that. He just wasn't into the same things that boys, or in fact, girls, at his school were. There was no obsession with PlayStation versus Xbox, or having discussions over who would win a fight between Hulk and Ironman, (which would obviously be the Hulk. Why? Because he's the Hulk of course. Duh!). There was no TikTok, Snapchat or Instagram. He didn't rush home every night and settle down in front of Disney+ or Netflix while his mum cooked his tea. He wasn't the slightest bit interested in having a mobile phone or playing on his mum's iPad, and he never brought any friends home to play. This was always a cause for concern with his mum, who would whine at him, 'You need to find some friends, Jack. It's unhealthy what you're doing. Grandad won't be around forever you know.'

And that was exactly why Jack liked, more than anything in the entire world, to spend time with his grandad. Whether it was tinkering with broken machinery, looking at old photographs and hearing the stories behind them, or winding Jack's grandma up to the point where her head nearly exploded. On one occasion, Jack and his grandad had rearranged her gnomes whilst she was out shopping. One, who had a hand raised, was placed on the wall facing the pavement, making it look like he was waving at passers-by. Another was holding a fishing rod, with a garden fairy hanging from the end of it, over a prickly bush. And finally, two gnomes were placed facing each other, as if they were having a fight, with an outer circle of garden decorations forming a crowd around them. An hour later, the door burst open to reveal Jean Finch standing there with a bag of shopping in each hand and an angry look on her face.

'Oh, hello love, how was your morning?' asked Jack's grandad, continuing to leaf through the sports section of his newspaper.

'Herbert! Would you please explain what you have done with my gnomes!'

'Me? What am I supposed to have done now?' Herbert asked, before standing and going to peek outside. 'Well, would you look at that? How odd!'

Jack's grandma didn't say a word. She dropped the shopping, snatched the newspaper from her husband's hands, and pursed her lips together as she rolled it up.

'Now, Jean, don't do anything silly,' Herbert protested, raising his hands in defence. 'Not in front of the boy!'

Jean finished rolling up the newspaper, raised it in the air, and whacked her husband on the head with it. Herbert laughed and ran for the safety of the kitchen, much to Jack's amusement.

'Help! I'm getting attacked by a crazy old woman with a plastic hip and a glass eye!' Herbert shouted, covering his head, and giggling all the way, while his annoyed wife chased after him with the rolled-up newspaper raised above her head.

Jack loved his grandad and knew that not a single boy, or girl, in the world had one like him. His grandad was unique. Oh, millions of children would claim theirs was the best, or the most exciting, or the most supportive. Jack would often hear them, either at school or on TV, and he would simply smirk and shake his head. That was because they were all wrong. None of them had the best grandad in the world. Well, they couldn't, because Jack did, and there was no denying it ... especially after what he'd discovered at the bottom of his grandparents' garden, some four years ago.

2008

CHAPTER ONE

The Garage

It was a glorious summer's day without a cloud in the sky. Birds were chirping in the trees and the smell of freshly cut grass hung in the air. There was a gentle breeze circling Jack's grandparents' garden: perfect conditions for flying his paper aeroplane from one end to the other. Jack was running around making combat noises and pretending he was embroiled in a battle during the war. As each assault intensified, he pulled his arm back and launched the plane as far as he could – being careful to keep it away from his grandma's flowers and the fishpond.

After twenty minutes of intense battling, Jack launched the plane with more force than he intended. It flew higher than normal, and a sudden gust of wind carried it straight through the open window of his grandad's garage. Jack threw his hands up to his face and spun around to see if his grandparents were watching, but thankfully they were busy in the kitchen. Jack could hear them shouting at each other – and then came his grandad's booming laugh. He was obviously winding Jack's grandma up, again. Jack turned and ran towards the garage. His heart began to race. He needed to get his plane back before he was caught.

His grandma had warned him never to go into grandad's 'man cave', as she called it, because it was full of dangerous tools and chemicals. Jack had promised he never would. She had smiled and ruffled his hair, given him a cookie and told him he was a good boy.

Jack paused at the garage door. What would his grandparents say if they caught him? He had made a promise to his grandma, and he knew you should never break a promise. Jack glanced back. The garden was empty, except for a couple of birds pecking at the grass, trying to disturb the worms. Suddenly, the neighbour's cat jumped over the fence, encouraging the birds to take flight. Jack turned his attention back to his task as the cat proceeded to clean itself. If he was quick, nobody would know he had been in here, and he could go back to playing with his plane. Little did he know, but he would be gone for far longer than he imagined.

Jack raised his hand and slowly wrapped his fingers around the rusty handle. With a gentle twist, he eased the door open. The hinges creaked, causing his heart to race even faster. He pushed it open just enough to allow him to peek inside. The light, entering through the grease-stained window through which Jack's plane had entered, gave a soft glow to the front of the garage, although the rear remained shrouded in darkness. The garage had a strange smell – one that Jack recognised instantly: the same musky aroma that clung to his grandad after he had spent a whole afternoon in here.

Jack stepped inside and looked around. Underneath the window was a long wooden bench. Scraps of wood, pots of paint, tools and cloths were piled on top. A large vice was fixed to the far end of the bench, a steel pipe clenched in its jaws. On the adjoining wall were several storage brackets; drills, chisels, and a variety of saws hung there, lined up and ready for action. Next to these was a shelf containing boxes of assorted fixings, screws, nails, tacks and clips.

Jack stood still and took in the garage. He'd never seen anything like it. He wondered why his grandad spent so much time in here, disappearing at every given opportunity. This was something Herbert was especially inclined to do if he had annoyed Jack's grandma to the point where she kicked him out for the afternoon. Once, on returning from a long spell in the garage, grandma had asked what he had been doing for so long. Herbert simply smiled and said, 'Having fun, Jean. You should try it sometime. You never know, you might even enjoy it.' He had winked at Jack and then quickly ducked, just as Jean threw a tea towel at her husband.

Jack cast his eyes over the cluttered bench, but his plane was nowhere to be seen. He carefully made his way towards the tools on the far wall, ensuring he didn't get too close. His grandma was right: they looked extremely dangerous. He glanced to his left and peered through the window. The coast was still clear, nobody was coming to look for him. His eyes settled on something that filled the middle of the garage. How had he not noticed this when he first entered? He moved towards the old, clapped-out car which was covered in dust and obviously had not been driven for years. The tyres were flat, and there was no driver's door or roof, but that was by design. It was one of those racing cars you climbed into. Jack crept closer and inspected the inside. The seat was ripped in several places, and the inner padding was attempting to force its way out. Spots of erosion were visible in the footwell, the steering wheel was broken, and the damaged windows of the dials were covered in dust and grime. Above the dashboard was a small windscreen that was cracked and covered in green slime, collected over many years of neglect.

Jack slowly worked his way to the back of the old banger, trailing a hand along it as he went. On the rear right-hand side there was some faded lettering. He moved closer to try to read it. He thought he could make out the letter H but couldn't be sure. Jack imagined the car was once a bright red colour, the same shade as fire engines, but now it was so faded it was hard to tell.

The hinges of the garage door squeaked, and sunlight burst through the open doorway. Jack froze: eyes wide, heart racing. He was going to be in big trouble if he got caught, but there was no way he could escape. He needed to hide, but where? He spun around to look for somewhere suitable and spotted his paper plane lying on a large green sheet, next to the double doors at the far end of the garage. The squeaking returned as the door was closed, shutting out the daylight once more.

Jack scurried over, picked up his plane, and hastily pulled himself under the sheet, immediately discovering two steps that led to a thick black door hidden behind it, which was slightly ajar. He was apprehensive about going through the door, but the sound of footsteps approaching left him with little choice. He sneaked through the gap and gasped.

Jack was inside a capsule that reminded him of the Millennium Falcon's cockpit in the Star Wars films. He took in every aspect of the contraption. On the far side was a dashboard that looked like a control centre. Red and green buttons, which were gently flashing away, filled the left-hand side, with numerous dials and switches contained on the right. Wires and cables protruded from underneath the dashboard and ran along the floor to a circular table in the middle, which was surrounded by three large leather chairs. The table had a digital clock sitting in the middle of it. Each of the six digits displayed a yellow zero. Next to this was a digital map of the world. A single green dot was pulsing away in the bottom right-hand corner.

The footsteps were now right outside. Jack spun around, looking for somewhere to hide before it was too late. The sound of flapping filled his ears as the green sheet was lifted. He was about to be discovered and would be in big trouble. But then he noticed a small compartment behind one of the chairs. It was just big enough to conceal a seven-year-old boy. Jack dropped to his knees and crawled inside the compartment, pulling himself in as tight as he could. The shuffling feet entered and then the door was slammed shut. Jack heard a psst! followed by a familiar sound as his grandad began to chuckle.

'Here we go again,' Herbert said to himself. 'Time to disappear and have some fun for the afternoon. A bit of time to myself without her nagging me. The only question is, where do you want to go today, Herbie? So many choices, but there's only one contender. I think I want to nip back and see the boys.'

Jack stuck his head out just enough to see what his grandad was doing and watched him fiddling with something on the digital display.

'Thirtieth of July, 1966,' muttered Herbert.

When he had finished adjusting the dials and switches, there was a sequence of beeps and an audible click as a green light illuminated above the dashboard, presumably confirming selection. Herbert settled into a chair, pulled two straps over his shoulders and clicked them in place. Next, he reached under his seat and removed a bright red helmet, which had a white number ten on both sides.

Without realising, Jack had edged out even further to get a closer look. His eyes were like saucers, and he was holding his breath, as if that would stop him being spotted.

With the helmet strap firmly fastened under his chin, Herbert dropped his right hand and pressed a button located on the arm of his seat. As it started to glow, he reached up and pulled down the goggles that were resting on the top of his helmet.

Jack felt his heart race faster than ever as the beeping intensified, and the capsule began to shake. What was happening? How was he supposed to get out of here now? He had been hoping to hide until his grandad left, but that wasn't going to be possible now. In his panic, Jack edged out even further, not knowing what to do.

Herbert was looking at the digital display, laughing and rubbing his hands together. He was clearly very excited about something. At the same time, the roaring became louder, the beeping more protracted and the shaking more violent, causing

Jack to gasp. Herbert looked around sharply. His smile instantly faded, his laughter stopped, and his face turned white.

'Oh no,' Herbert cried. His gaze was fixed on his grandson, crouched behind the seat opposite. Jack's tear-filled eyes were wide open, his bottom lip was quivering, and his paper plane was tightly clenched in his tiny shaking hands.

CHAPTER TWO

Blast Off

Herbert unclicked his seatbelt, rushed over to Jack, picked him up and settled him into the seat he had been hiding behind.

'What are you doing in here, Jack? My God, she'll string me up if she finds out.' Herbert's voice was shaking almost as much as his hands. 'How did you get in?'

The whirring became louder, and the shaking increased.

Herbert pulled the straps over Jack's head and clicked them in place. He gave one hard tug to ensure his grandson was safe, stood back, and shook his head. 'This is not good, but I can't do anything about it now. You sit tight. I need to finish what I'm doing.'

Jack let his eyes wander. The digital display in the middle of the central console, which had been showing six zeros, now contained two yellow numbers on the left-hand side: a number four, followed by a seven. No – now it was a six ... a five ... a four ... Jack watched the digits. The number four disappeared and was replaced with a three. The numbers were counting down.

'Wh-wh-what happens when it reaches zero, Grandad?' Jack asked, unable to take his eyes off the display.

Herbert looked at his quivering grandson and smiled. 'When that reaches zero, you must make sure you're holding on tight, because you are going to experience something truly spectacular.'

'Will we be okay?'

'We're going to be fine, Jack. Don't worry; I won't let any harm come to you. Your grandmother would have my guts for garters if anything happened to her *precious boy*.'

Herbert slipped his own helmet onto Jack's head and fastened it as tightly as he could. He tied a knot in the straps of the goggles to ensure they would fit and slipped them over Jack's eyes. The display read twenty seconds. It was nearly time. A psst! sound, like a rush of air escaping from a valve, bubbled up from underneath.

Herbert jumped back into the seat opposite, but there was no helmet for him. So he hurriedly reached into the pocket of his coat, removed a white carrier bag, and pulled it over his head, tying it beneath his chin.

Jack's eyes were darting around. The whirring had increased further. A glance sideways.

The display was down to seven … six …

'Now, hold on tight,' Herbert said. 'This will all be worth it, Jack, my boy. Okay?'

Jack didn't say anything. He simply nodded.

Two … one …

Then, for the first, but not the last time, Jack's ears were filled with two words he had only ever heard on TV before.

'Blast off!' shouted Herbert.

They began moving. Not up, not left, not right, forwards or backwards. They actually plunged down. Jack held his breath as the machine shook from side to side.

'You okay?' asked Herbert.

Jack nodded, his eyes still wide open. He wasn't sure if he'd blinked once since he sneaked in through the solid black door. He must have, but he couldn't remember.

'Look,' Herbert said, pointing to Jack's left.

Jack noticed a window. He gasped and his eyes darted from the window to his grandad and back again. They were moving through the cold, damp earth, penetrating deep underground. Worms wriggled around on the other side of the glass as the machine pushed its way onwards, until finally slowing and coming to a stop. Had they broken down? Were they going to die, deep underground? What was his mum going to say? Not that Jack would find out.

'Now comes the fun bit,' said Herbert.

The machine gave a loud rumble and they began moving again, this time in a different direction: they were climbing.

Jack sat, mesmerised. Daylight filtered in through the window. The earth piled against the glass, fell away as they continued to climb, making way for more bright sunshine to illuminate the inside of the capsule. Spears of orange light pierced the three porthole windows situated opposite the rectangular window, highlighting the digital timer that was now displaying six numbers: 30:07:66.

Jack looked questioningly at his grandad, trying to make sense of what he was seeing.

'I'll explain everything later, Jack. I promise.'

Jack simply nodded.

The machine rumbled louder.

'Right, here we go. Hang on tight. Once we're up high it'll be plain sailing. We can't afford to be seen in this thing, so the take-off is a bit quick.'

Jack gripped the armrests. He didn't want any nasty accidents.

The lights on the dashboard began flashing, a *whoop-whoop* sound reverberated around the room, and then, without warning, they shot high into the air, leaving the cold, damp earth behind.

Jack felt his stomach lurch. He was gripping the armrests so tightly that his forearms ached, but he daren't let go. Jack looked over at the window and saw nothing but a blue blur as they continued to soar through the sky. White mist billowed past the window, giving the impression they had hit a patch of fog, but Jack knew what it was: clouds.

Their speed decreased and Jack puffed out his cheeks. He sat there calming himself down and recovering from the heart-pounding experience. He released his grip on the armrests and wiped his sweaty palms on his trousers. He was so relieved that they had slowed down and were now floating freely, high in the sky. He had no idea what was going on, but his panicking had been replaced with excitement. Jack giggled at the sight of his grandad sitting opposite with the white carrier bag, which he had removed from his pocket earlier, tied under his chin.

'Think I might be starting a new fashion,' Herbert said, wobbling his head.

Jack smiled and tried his hardest to relax, although he found it difficult. Soaring above the clouds was not the most relaxing afternoon he had ever spent with his grandad, but it was certainly different.

CHAPTER THREE

Herbert Explains

Once the initial shock was over, Jack breathed a sigh of relief.

'Enjoy that?' asked Herbert.

Jack nodded. He was no longer worried about what was happening, although it was a good job he wasn't scared of heights or he would have been freaking out.

'Is it okay to undo my seatbelt now, Grandad?'

'You want to look out of the window, eh?'

Jack nodded.

Herbert unclipped his belt and helped Jack with his straps.

'There you go. Just don't get too close to the window. There's a trapdoor in front of it that's a little temperamental. It has a tendency to fly open on its own.'

Jack sat rigid. He no longer wanted to go and look out of the window.

His grandad laughed, 'I'm joking. There's no trapdoor in here!'

Herbert took Jack's hand and walked him to the window. The clear blue sky was broken up by a few fluffy clouds. Jack tried to spot something he recognised, but it was impossible from this height. He craned his neck and looked to the right, but all he could see was the sea stretching out for miles in front of them.

Jack turned and looked at his grandad, who was smiling, his eyes firmly fixed on his grandson.

'I suppose you want an explanation?'

Jack nodded.

'I always planned to tell you about this time machine when you were—'

'This is a time machine?' Jack blurted out.

'Indeed, it is.'

'Wow. That's so cool! Did you build it, Grandad?'

Herbert shook his head. 'No. I was always going to tell you about it when you were older. I guess time has jumped forward a little bit now.'

As he walked back to his chair, Herbert removed the bag from his head, placed it back inside his coat pocket and popped his favourite newsboy cap back on.

'Come,' he said, patting Jack's chair. 'Take a seat and I'll explain.'

Jack sat down and faced his grandad. Herbert cleared his throat, leant forward, and went straight into story mode. He'd always been a good storyteller, ever since Jack was little. He would make up funny characters with silly voices and give them all weird names. He never read from a book, as he once explained, 'Story books are okay, Jack, but where's the imagination in reading words on a page that somebody else has written? You may not like the characters, or you may find the story boring, and there's nothing you can do about it. But make up your own story and you can change it or add characters as you go. That's so much more fun.'

Jack enjoyed reading books, but his grandad's stories were so much better, especially when he included his grandma in them. Of course, she was always the baddie, or a wicked witch with a scraggly beard, much to her annoyance.

'It all started a long time ago,' Herbert began. 'I used to like practical lessons in school, and I was always tinkering about with all sorts of stuff outside of class. I had a real love for mechanics and finding out how things worked.' His gaze fixed on the floor for a second, concentrating, while he recalled the event from memory. 'When your mum was a little older than you are now, she went on a school trip to a museum. There were so many children going that they asked if any parents could help out. Your grandma thought it might be fun for me to go, so she put my name down. I was certain they wouldn't want me on the trip, particularly all the snobby mums who always looked down their noses at me, but for some reason I was chosen to go.'

Jack said nothing but stared at his grandad as he continued with the story.

'Your mum didn't want me hanging around with her, so I ended up in another group, which suited me just fine. Anyway, as we were walking around the museum, I got a bit distracted. I wandered towards a huge display of World War II artefacts, while the children were listening to a talk on dinosaur bones. I was reading all about the magnificent Spitfire planes used during the war, when I felt somebody standing beside me. I turned to find one of the museum workers looking at the display. He was a funny-looking fella who reminded me of my old science teacher. His hair was jet black with a parting on the right-hand side.

It looked like it was glued to his head due to the amount of gel he'd applied.'

This caused Jack to giggle. He had seemingly forgotten they were soaring above the clouds in a time machine.

'He was wearing a long brown dustcoat that smelt like it had come back from the war itself. Around his neck, tucked under the collar of his crisp white shirt, was the most colourful bow tie I'd ever seen. Honestly, he looked very strange. And, to think, your grandma says I dress weird,' Herbert said with a huff. 'Then, without looking in my direction, the man spoke to me.'

'What did he say?' asked Jack.

'It's embedded in my mind. I'll never forget our conversation. He said, "Nobody in here can imagine what we went through during the war."' Herbert screwed up his face and hunched his shoulders, mimicking the look of the museum worker. He couldn't tell a story without being in character mode. Jack was unsure if this was for his benefit, or his grandad's.

Herbert continued. 'I turned towards him, but he wasn't looking at me. He was lost in among the artefacts safely protected behind the thick glass in front of us, but he carried on talking to me. He said, "We lived in fear every single day, expecting the alarms and the warnings to sound. And when they finally did scream through the sky, bedlam broke out. Men, women and children all frantically ran for cover, knowing they were coming.'"

'*They*?' asked Jack, eyes wide, lost in the tale.

Herbert looked into the innocent eyes of his seven-year-old grandson. 'The Germans, Jack. The Germans were coming. They were coming to attack and bomb England. Sirens would sound, warning everyone to stop what they were doing and run to their shelters. And then the sky would turn black as wave after wave of their planes, the Luftwaffe, soared across the sky. A whirring sound would fill the air as they dropped their bombs on the poor, innocent people below.'

Jack was engrossed in the story. 'Why?'

'Because they were following orders from their evil leader, Adolf Hitler. He wanted to rule the world, but, unfortunately for him, we had one thing they didn't.'

'What did we have?'

'Winston Churchill,' Herbert said proudly.

'Whoa! Was he a pilot?' asked Jack.

'*A pilot*? Goodness, no! He was our prime minister. And a bloomin' good one, too. Anyway,' Herbert said, waving a dismissive hand, 'this man said the most peculiar thing to me.'

'What did he say?' Jack asked, so close to the edge of his seat it was amazing he didn't fall off.

Herbert leant forwards and smiled. 'He said, "Do you want to see for yourself?"'

Jack paused for a moment, trying to understand what his grandad was saying. 'Want to see what?'

'The war, Jack. He asked if I wanted to see the London Blitz during World War II.'

Jack was stunned. He didn't know if this was one of his grandad's jokes, or if he was being serious. There really was no way of telling. The only thing Jack knew was that, either way, it was all very exciting.

'What did you say to him, Grandad?'

Herbert sat back in his seat, crossed his legs, and smiled again.

'Why, I said yes, of course.'

They continued to sweep across the Cornish skyline. Jack had no idea what to make of this whole situation. Was his grandad playing some sort of weird trick on him? Was the window really just a TV screen, rigged up to show a passing scene? His grandad may well be telling the truth about the war and the man in the museum, but he was the best storyteller in the world, so Jack was still dubious. For all he knew, the door could soon burst open to reveal his grandma standing there with a stern look on her face and her finger – the 'Finch finger' as it was affectionately known – wagging, berating him for disobeying her in venturing into the garage. Jack wasn't sure if that was the case – and even if it was, he didn't care. He was spending time with his most favourite person in the world, and that's all that mattered.

'Grandad?'

'Yes, my boy?'

'If this really is a time machine, how did you get it? I mean, you're clever, but only at winding grandma up, so I don't think you could've built it … and if you didn't, then how did you get it? Because, if I'm honest, I don't believe you. I mean, mum says she's impressed you can tie your own shoelaces, because you are the clumsiest man she knows, and she lives with my dad! So, building your own time machine is not something you could do,' said Jack, trying his hardest not to burst out laughing as shock consumed his grandad's face.

'Your mum said that, did she?' asked Herbert, shaking his head in disbelief. 'Well, you're right, I didn't build it. I obtained it from the man in the museum after he asked me to follow him. At first I was a bit unsure. I turned to check the children were still being entertained by the guide and wouldn't miss me for ten minutes. All was fine, so I followed him.'

Jack settled in his seat for the next part of grandad's story.

'He headed towards a thick brown door in the corner. There was a silver chain hanging loosely across the doorway with a *No Entry* sign attached to it. He pushed the door open, stepped over the chain, and disappeared into the darkness. A cool breeze rushed out and brushed across my face just before the door closed. I stood there thinking for a while. I knew I shouldn't really follow a man I'd never met before into a potentially dangerous situation, but I was intrigued. So I checked behind me before pushing the door open and walking into the darkness waiting for me.'

'Were you not scared?' asked Jack.

'Why? Because it was dark? No, I'm used to the dark, especially with how tight your grandma is with turning lights on! Honestly, she's a pain, always trying to save money on electricity. Mind you, at least I can hardly see her face when it's dark,' he chuckled.

'No, I mean, there could've been anything down there. He may have been leading you into a trap. There could have been a monster down there or anything,' said Jack.

Herbert laughed. 'Jack, my boy, there were no monsters down there. I could make another joke about your grandma, but this is meant to be my escape pod from her!'

'I wouldn't have followed him,' Jack said. 'I would have been too scared.'

The conversation was interrupted when the time machine lurched suddenly to the left. Jack gripped the armrests for dear life. His eyes widened and he searched his grandad's face, looking for confirmation that there was nothing to worry about and that they were not about to start plummeting towards the earth. The faint sound of squawking noises could just be made out over the rumbling of the engines as they worked even harder to lift the machine higher. Herbert glanced over at the window. Jack followed his gaze. There was nothing to see but the burning orange glow emanating from the engines, shimmering and roaring away.

'What's ha-ha-happening, Grandad?' asked Jack.

'It's nothing to worry about. It will pass in a minute,' replied Herbert.

Flapping sounds joined the squawking outside. The machine juddered and then dropped. Jack felt tears prickling his eyes and his stomach flipped over. Was this going to be the end? Were they about to crash?

There then came a *thud-thud-thud* against the side of the time machine, making Jack jump. His eyes were like saucers as he glanced from one side to the other, switching between the window and his grandad.

And then, as quickly as it had started, it stopped. The engines died down, the orange glow faded and all that could be seen out of the window was a flock of birds, rapidly disappearing in the distance.

'Bloomin' things. Always get in the way, they do. Anyone would think they own the skies,' Herbert said, smiling, before leaning forwards and ruffling Jack's hair. 'You're braver than you look. You okay?'

Jack was shaken, but nodded.

'Good boy. Anyway, where were we? Ah, yes. I was following the museum man and wondering what hid in the darkness behind the old museum door.'

1982

CHAPTER FOUR

Meeting William Bertrand

The door closed, leaving Herbert in complete darkness, save for a dim light somewhere down below. The dull echoing of the museum man's shoes floated through the air as he descended the stairs. The air was damp. Herbert could feel dust particles landing on his skin.

He grabbed the handrail and followed the sound of footsteps. It was surprising how many steps there were, considering the museum entrance was at street level.

He eventually reached the bottom and noticed the faint light was coming from a lamp on a desk in the corner.

The man he'd followed was standing at the desk, shuffling paperwork. He didn't look up as Herbert approached, but carried on with what he was doing. It was as if Herbert wasn't there. But then he said something that made Herbert freeze.

'About time you turned up, Herbie.'

Herbert stopped dead. 'Do I know you?'

'I very much doubt it.'

'Then how do you know my name?' Herbert asked, moving towards the desk.

'Lucky guess,' the man chuckled, still not looking up. 'No, I don't know you ... Well, not as such. But I do know everything about you.'

Herbert watched the strange man finish tidying his desk. Was he an old schoolteacher? Had he been involved with one of Herbert's various sports clubs over the years? Had their paths crossed in some form and Herbert had forgotten where or when? He didn't think so. In fact, he was certain he'd never seen the man before.

'Codswallop!' Herbert said, offended that this strange man thought he knew all about him. How could he? It was like the man said: they'd never met.

'I think you'll find it's not *codswallop*, Herbie. I could tell you many things about your past. Things

I couldn't possibly know unless I knew you,' the man said, finally looking up.

Herbert stepped closer. 'Listen here. I don't know what you sprinkled on your breakfast this morning, but we've never seen each other before. I think I'd remember meeting someone with that much gel in his hair!'

'Now, Herbie,' said the man, 'don't go being like that. I was hoping we'd become friends.'

'I think that's highly unlikely,' said Herbert and turned to walk away. 'Anyway, I'm going to go back up to the children now. Have fun in your little dungeon down here ... Oh, and another thing. You might wanna get some lighting installed. Bit dangerous with just that lamp.'

Herbert reached the bottom of the steps and then the old man said something that made him stop and turn.

'How's Jean?'

Herbert paused with one hand resting on the cold railing. 'What did you say?'

'I asked how your lovely wife is.'

The penny dropped, and Herbert breathed a sigh of relief. Of course, he must be a family friend from his wife's side. Now it made sense. He must have recognised Herbert from a photograph, and Jean had probably explained all about her childish, annoying, loveable-rogue of a husband. That must be it!

'Ah, so, you know me through the wife?' smiled Herbert.

'Nope. Never met her,' the man replied with a shake of the head. 'And your little girl, Jasmine, how's she doing in school? I saw her up there walking around. She looked to be having a wonderful time.'

Herbert had heard enough. 'Alright, you've got ten seconds to explain what you're going on about and how you know my family, or I swear I'm going to–'

'Herbie, relax ...' the man said, raising his hands, palms outwards. 'There's no need to be so hostile. I'm no harm to you. I mean, look at me: I'm twice your age.'

Herbert eyeballed the museum worker. He couldn't leave now; he was too intrigued to find out how this stranger knew him and his family.

'Look, follow me over here and I'll explain everything,' the man said. 'Trust me, Herbie. It'll be to your benefit, I promise you.'

The stranger made his way past the dimly illuminated desk and disappeared. Herbert stood, thinking, for a second and then walked back over to the desk.

'Okay,' agreed Herbert. It was all he could think to say in the situation.

'Good,' came the man's voice from the shadows.

The dull clunk of a lever reverberated around the vast, empty space, which flooded with light as four huge lamps, high above them, burst into life. Herbert raised his hands to protect his retinas from being burnt out by the intense light.

After a few seconds, he lowered his hands and looked up. Herbert stood, open-mouthed, looking like he'd been frozen in time. The sound of tapping shoes approached. The large basement was completely empty, apart from the desk, and what looked like a large wooden hut in the middle of the room.

'What's this thing?' asked Herbert, looking at the contraption.

'I thought you'd be impressed,' the man said, sidling up next to him.

Herbert turned. Now that he was smiling, the man had a kind, yet wrinkled face. Warm emerald eyes burnt brightly behind thick black glasses. His bow tie was positioned perfectly straight and centred inside the wings of his crisp white shirt. His hands were thrust into the pockets of his dustcoat.

The old man smiled, removed his right hand from his pocket, and offered it to Herbert. 'William Bertrand.'

'Herbert Finch. But you already know that,' said Herbert, taking the stranger's hand and shaking it.

'Indeed I do. So, I suppose you want to know about this little beauty?'

'*Little*?' Herbert asked. 'I wouldn't exactly call it *little*. What is it?'

'This is the reason I know all about you, Herbie, and your family, too. This is the reason I can see whatever I want, whenever I want. It's the reason I can fly around the world and be back before that clock,' added William, pointing at a large gold clock on the wall, 'has moved by a single second. You see, this is a time machine.'

'*A time machine*?' snorted Herbert. 'Are you pulling my leg? Has Jean put you up to this?'

'Not at all,' replied William. 'Nobody knows about this. Well, nobody except you, that is.'

'Right. Now you're confusing me. You mean to tell me that nobody from the museum has ever been down here?'

'Nope,' said William, removing a pipe from his coat pocket, offering it up to his mouth and clamping his teeth down on it.

'*Nobody*? Not even the museum manager?'

'My dear boy, there's one thing you need to understand,' advised William, sounding like a ventriloquist with the pipe clenched between his teeth.

'What's that?'

William Bertrand removed the pipe and leant in closer. He placed a hand on Herbert's shoulder before whispering in his ear. 'I am the museum manager.'

CHAPTER FIVE

The Time Machine

The air in the basement had turned ice cold. A time machine. How could this man, who claimed to be the museum manager, but looked more like a cleaner, own a time machine? Where did it come from? Was it real, or was this one big joke? It couldn't be a time machine. It just couldn't. Could it? Surely those contraptions only existed in films, not in real life. William was definitely making fun of him.

'So, what is this thing, then?' asked Herbert. 'I mean, what is it *really*?'

'I told you. It's a time machine.'

'Of course it is! You keep taking those pills! You'll be alright in a week or two, I'm sure!' joked

Herbert. 'There's no such thing as a time machine. Except in the movies, of course, and ... well, I'm not being funny, but you don't look like a movie star.'

William smiled. 'Fair enough. I didn't expect you to believe me.'

'I'm sorry, but it's the most absurd thing I've ever heard, and I've been married for over ten years!'

William shook his head and scratched it with the mouthpiece of his pipe.

'So, you're the museum manager?' Herbert asked, changing the subject.

'Indeed, I am,' replied William, standing tall and puffing his chest out. 'I've held the position for nearly forty years.'

'And have you ... erm ... had this down here the whole time?' asked Herbert, gesticulating towards the time machine.

William chuckled as he answered. 'Well, I obtained it some thirty years ago. It's not the sort of thing you can go and purchase in a store ... Once everything was in place, and I was confident enough, I tried it out.'

'What do you mean, *tried it out*?' asked Herbert.

'Well, I went back, of course. That is what it's meant to do, after all.'

'*Went back? Went back* where?'

William sighed and rubbed his forehead. 'Back in time of course. It's a—'

'—time machine, yes, so you keep saying!' Herbert interrupted, shaking his head.

He turned and looked towards the three flights of steps leading back to the museum. They were now perfectly illuminated, but the room still had a sinister air to it. There were dark patches where the lighting from the dome fittings couldn't reach, along with spindly shadows created by the railings. Even though the voices in his head were telling him to get away from this old man and out of his creepy basement, Herbert's eyes were drawn towards the mysterious contraption.

He studied the perfect craftsmanship before stepping closer and placing a hand against the smooth, polished wood, as if he was calming a nervous animal. Despite the damp air circulating the basement, the wood was warm to the touch. Herbert caressed the grain, feeling its beauty under his fingertips. From the texture, he could tell it was thick, sturdy and well built. The heads of silver rivets and screws, which had been used to build the machine, were all equidistantly spaced, giving the machine uniformity in its construction. On one side were three small round windows, like portholes on a ship, inserted into gold frames, which sat flush against the wooden panels.

Herbert reached up and rapped his knuckles against one of them. Like the wood, he could tell from the dull thud they made that the glass was very thick indeed.

He reached the opposite side, where there was another window, a rectangular one. It stretched the length of one side. Herbert didn't touch the window this time but he did try to peer inside; all he could see was the same inky darkness that had occupied the basement before William had turned on the lights.

Herbert thrust his hands into his pockets and looked directly at the museum manager. 'Well, I have no idea what it is, but I must say, the craftsmanship is exceptional.'

'You still don't believe it's a time machine, do you?'

'No ... No, I don't, I'm afraid. Time machines don't exist!'

William lifted a small flap situated beside the door, revealing a blue numerical keypad, and entered a sequence of numbers. Each one was met with an audible *beep!*, and then there was a *psst!* sound as he opened the door. William didn't say a word. He simply climbed the two metal steps leading to the door, pulled it open, stepped inside and disappeared from view.

Herbert stood there for a few seconds before throwing his arms in the air. 'Oh, what the hell,' he said and followed William inside the time machine hidden three floors beneath the museum.

Once inside, he closed the door and turned around. William was sitting in one of three chairs, smiling at him. Well, it looked like he was smiling, but his pipe was, once again, clenched between his teeth, so it looked like a semi-grimace.

'So, Herbie,' said William, removing the pipe from his mouth and displaying what was, in fact, the biggest smile. 'Where do you fancy going?'

Herbert stared back, his expression blank.

William removed the pipe and waved it around in the air. 'Pick an event from the past. Anything you want to see. First-hand. Not on TV, and not in the papers. Have a think about it and let me know … I'm in no rush.'

Herbert was sure William had lost his marbles, but he thought he may as well keep the doddery old fool happy. And besides, he was curious.

'This is your gadget,' emphasised Herbert, settling into the seat opposite, 'so you can choose.'

He knew this wasn't real. The silly old man was probably going to set it up and sit in his seat making rumbling noises and imitating the sounds of a rocket ship taking off. Presumably, they would then step outside and pretend they were wherever it was they were supposed to be.

He watched William fiddle with the dials on the dashboard before turning his attention to the central console.

William clapped his hands together and stared at Herbert. 'How do you fancy seeing something special?'

'What do you mean?'

'Well, we're in a museum, are we not?'

'Yes ... Well, kind of.'

'And you were interested in the artefacts on display. Yes?'

'Of course.'

'Well,' continued William, 'it seems perfectly clear to me where we should go for your first time-travelling experience.'

'Like I said,' barked Herbert, showing his frustration. 'This is your machine, so you take us where you think we should go, and I'll come along for the ride. How does that sound?'

'Sounds perfect.'

Herbert watched William set the dials on the digital display, which was showing six zeros. He almost felt sorry for him. William was obviously a few sandwiches short of a picnic, but this was clearly one of his pleasures in life, pretending he had a time machine, so Herbert was happy to indulge the old man.

William pressed a gently pulsing blue button on his armrest. 'Hold on tight!'

A whirring sound filled the air, and the machine began to rumble.

'You really have gone to town to make this feel realistic, William ... I'll give you that!'

William smiled, popped his pipe in his mouth and crossed his legs, his eyes firmly set on his passenger.

Herbert looked out of the large rectangular window, but something was wrong. It wasn't as big as it looked from the outside. He looked to the other side. The portholes were no bigger than golf balls. What was happening? All the windows had shrunk. Maybe it was one of those weird illusions.

He glanced at the digital display. The zeros were gone, replaced by another six digits: 08:05:41. What did those numbers signify? The whirring became louder, the rumbling fiercer and then the smell of smoke filled the machine.

Herbert glanced towards the window but there was nothing to see. His heart began to race. His hands were sweating and his breathing heavy. He had a terrible feeling he was in big trouble. Maybe William had been telling the truth all along. Maybe they were actually sitting in a real time machine. It couldn't be true. Could it?

The rumbling intensified, and Herbert looked across at William with pleading eyes. The museum manager just sat there, smiling, puffing away on his unlit pipe, clearly enjoying Herbert's discomfort.

He then removed the pipe, leant forward and muttered two words that made Herbert feel both scared and excited at the same time. 'Told you.'

William sat back, crossed his legs, and blew imaginary smoke above his head.

CHAPTER SIX

Liar

They'd now been sitting in the time machine for over ten minutes and Herbert was worried about the school trip. What were they going to think when the children discovered he'd disappeared? Even worse, what if something bad had happened to the group he'd been tasked with supervising? News would obviously filter back to the school, and he would be the talk of the presumptuous, hoity-toity mums.

He could handle all the looks, the stares, and the comments. He would even make a joke out of it. But what he wasn't looking forward to was trying to explain it all to his wife. Sweat was breaking out over Herbert's forehead at the mere thought of it.

'So, Herbie. How do you feel now?' asked a very smug-looking William. He was leaning back in his chair, holding the bowl end of his pipe as he puffed away on the mouthpiece. It looked very odd, considering it was still unlit.

'I still think this is some trick and in a minute that door will open, and we'll still be in the museum basement ...'

'You really think that's the case?'

'Yes, I do', answered Herbert. 'There's no way you've built a time machine. I may look stupid, but I'm cleverer than I look!'

William gave him a knowing nod, reached around and pressed a large bright button on the dashboard behind him, which made an audible click, followed by a *whap! whap!* sound. Herbert read the words written across it: 'Do not press this button when airborne!'

'In that case,' William said, pulling the pipe out of his mouth and motioning with the mouthpiece towards the thick black door, 'be my guest.'

'What do you mean?'

'Go ahead, open the door, go back into the basement, take the three flights of stairs and head back to the children. Maybe you'll be lucky, and they won't even know you've been gone. Give Jasmine a nice hug and then you can head back home ... Go on, be my guest!'

Herbert noted the intensity in William's eyes. If this was all a trick, then he was a damn good actor, he had to give him that. But this had to be a joke, didn't it? There was no way they were flying high above the clouds. Absolutely no way.

He glanced over at the rectangular window. It had increased in size and was now as big as when he had first seen it from the outside.

'Alright then,' declared Herbert.

'*Alright* what?'

'I'm going to leave.'

'Like I said, be my guest,' repeated William, extending his arm towards the door.

'Right. I guess I'll see you later,' said Herbert, placing his hand on the lever.

'Wait!' Came a shout from behind him.

Gotcha, thought Herbert. It felt like he'd just won a game of chicken. 'Yes?'

William was putting on a pair of goggles. 'I want to make sure I don't miss any of this. Once you open that door, it's going to get a bit blowy in here, so I want to protect my eyes and make sure I see it all. You might want to put yours on, too!'

'What?'

'Put these on,' William said, offering a second pair of goggles to Herbert.

'Tell you what, William. You're playing up to the part very well. Jean must've paid you a fortune!'

Herbert operated the lever and there was a *psst!* as the door flew open. A whooshing sound immediately filled his ears, and a rush of air entered the open doorway. Herbert tried his hardest to close it, but the pressure from the air pushing against the door made it impossible. He gripped onto the door frame.

He wasn't staring out at the cold museum basement as he expected, but the clear blue sky hundreds of metres above the ground.

Herbert started to panic. He needed to get back to his seat and clip himself in, but there was no chance. His eyes were streaming with water. Tears rolled down his cheeks and dribbled out of the open doorway – just as he would at any moment. Why had he not put on the stupid goggles? Or, more importantly, why had he not just believed it was all true and that this really was a time machine? Why did he always have to be right?

His squinting eyes darted around. There were lights flashing all over the dashboard and warning sounds beeping loudly. And yet, sitting there, right in the middle of it, was William, puffing on his pipe and smiling away, his eyes firmly fixed on the young man who, moments earlier, had thought he was nothing more than a silly old man.

And then, as Herbert tried to reach for his seat, it happened. The air rushing all around grabbed hold of him like a giant hand. It took ownership of his legs and began pulling him out of the open doorway. More air wrapped around his fingers and began prising them from the metal framework that Herbert held onto for dear life.

He glanced up and locked eyes with William. 'Please! Please help me!' yelled Herbert.

William removed the pipe from his mouth and gave an apologetic look. 'You should've believed me, Herbie. Have a nice flight!'

Herbert finally lost his grip and was sucked outside. The sound of William's laughter filled his ears as he hurtled towards the ground below.

Herbert descended at a rate of knots. His heart was banging against his ribcage, demanding to be let out. With his eyes streaming, his cheeks flapping about wildly and his face contorted by the rushing wind, he looked like a dog with his head stuck out of a car window. This was it. This was the end. This was how he was going to die! What would they say at his funeral? 'We're here to say goodbye to Herbert Finch, who was, without doubt, the most stubborn man in the whole of Cornwall. The silly old sausage always knew best. Well, not this time, Herbie!'

Something brushed past him. He didn't dare open his eyes. Then he felt a crushing sensation in his chest as the air exploded from his lungs. There was something underneath him. He was suspended in mid-air. He'd been saved. But how?

He brought his hands up and wiped the cold sweat from his face before glancing down. He was being carried above the rooftops of a town – his hometown – and was now, he estimated, about thirty metres from the ground. He turned his head and looked up. He'd been caught in a large cargo net attached to the underside of the time machine. And standing there, in the opening Herbert had been sucked out of only seconds earlier, was William. He raised his pipe and waved. Herbert, bewildered, nervously raised his hand and waved back. He was still breathless, his heart was still racing, but he was safe. For now.

Relief flooded his body as the net was winched upwards, until he noticed two red dots on the underside of the machine, gently glowing away. When they suddenly got brighter, he realised what they were: jet engines. Not as big as the commercial ones he'd seen before, but powerful enough to send the time machine shooting forwards at great speed.

Herbert gripped the net even tighter; he knew what was coming. The whirring was becoming unbearable as the orange glow intensified.

Oh dear God, no! He can't ... not yet, Herbert thought, wiping globules of saliva from his cheeks. He was willing the rope, that aided his return, to turn over faster and get him there before the inevitable happened.

Only ten more metres and he'd be back through the doorway. He was going to make it, surely! Sweat was running from Herbert now; he wasn't sure if it was from the whole situation, or the heat from the engines. And then, just when he thought he'd soon be back sitting in his chair, the engines rotated. The red fire was no longer pointing towards the ground, but towards the rear. As a result, the roaring became unbearable.

And then it happened. The engines exploded into life, and the machine shot forwards. Herbert clung on for dear life as he sped through the air. The wind rushed across his face, the ear-splitting roar of the engines filled his ears and the abrasive rope of the net pressed firmly against his face.

'Help me!' begged Herbert, his voice no more than a pathetic whimper.

CHAPTER SEVEN

Into The Past

'What are you laughing at? That wasn't funny,' Herbert said, tripping as he wrestled his burly frame out of the cargo net.

'Oh, it was. It made my day – and the look on your face was worth the risk!' laughed William.

'You could've killed me,' growled Herbert. 'You do know that, don't you? If the rope had snapped, I would've been a goner.'

In frustration, he turned and aimed a kick at the now empty net, but his foot caught in one of the holes and he stumbled, only just managing to stay upright by reaching for the back of his empty seat.

William stuck the pipe in his mouth and bit down hard to avoid laughing any harder. 'Oh, we were only going at full speed for a couple of minutes. I had to get us away from the onlookers.'

'*Onlookers*?' asked Herbert.

'Can't have anyone finding out about this,' replied William, raising his arms and waving them around.

Herbert slumped in his seat and folded his arms. The shock of flying in a cargo net thirty metres above the ground was easing, but he was still annoyed.

William asked, 'So ... believe me now, do you?'

Herbert cast his eyes downwards and huffed.

William sighed before turning to the dashboard. 'Now, let's get back to what we were doing before you played silly buggers and tried to kill yourself.'

'I didn't try to kill myself,' Herbert said, unfolding his arms and sitting upright.

William didn't even turn around to answer. 'Oh, sorry! Normal to open doors of high-flying aircraft, is it?'

'*High-flying aircraft*? More like a glorified garden shed!' Herbert scowled.

'*Garden shed*, you say?'

'Yes.'

'Very well. Are we in the air?' asked William.

'What?'

'Just answer the question. Are we soaring through the air?'

'Yes, but I don't see–'

'And are we moving through the clouds?'

'Yes …'

'Do we have jet engines propelling us forwards?'

'Well, yes, but–'

'And it has passengers, yes?'

'The two of us, I suppose–'

'I'll take that as another yes.'

William finished fiddling with the dials and spun around. 'So, just to clarify. One: we're flying high in the air. Two: there are powerful jet engines aiding our journey, and three: there are passengers onboard. Sounds like an aircraft to me! But please, Herbie, explain why, in your eyes, we're not in an aircraft?'

William paused, peered over the top of his glasses and waited for a response.

Herbert said nothing. Here he was, a man in his mid-forties, being reprimanded by a pensioner.

After a moment of awkward silence, Herbert changed the subject. 'So, how does this actually work, then?'

'How does *what* work?' William asked, frowning and tapping his pipe on the armrest.

'You know, the whole time-travelling thingy?'

William raised his pipe and scratched his head with the mouthpiece. 'Well, in order for us to travel, we need to enter a doorway in time ... a portal, if you will.'

'*A portal*?'

William nodded. 'Yes. Once we set the date on this thing,' he said, tapping the top of the digital clock, 'and activate the system, the transportation portal will open, allowing us to transfer safely. We can then sit back and enjoy the journey. The time machine will do the hard work for us.'

'And what about returning? What happens if the portal vanishes? What happens then?'

William smiled. 'Don't worry. The portal will remain open. I assure you, there's no need to panic. I've travelled many times over the years and have never encountered any problems with getting back home.'

'Well–' Herbert began, but was interrupted by an ear-piercing alarm that came bursting from the dashboard.

Whap! Whap! Whap! Whap!

William reached across and pressed a button, which stopped the uncomfortable ringing.

'Perfect timing!' said William.

A flash of light burst through the window. Herbert rushed over to get a closer look, but all he could see was a mixture of the brightest colours: red, blue, orange, turquoise, silver and gold. The whirring and rumbling returned, more aggressive than before. The sky became dark, increasing the intense glare of the lights. He flashed a look at William, who was sitting in his chair, a picture of tranquillity, smiling away. Herbert continued looking for something to pull him back to reality – because this wasn't real, was it?

'What's happening to us?' he asked.

'You might want to strap yourself in – this could get a bit bumpy,' replied William.

'What could? What have you done?'

'Why, Herbert, we're going back to World War II, of course,' William tutted. 'How many times do I have to tell you?'

The whirring continued, urging Herbert to hurry up. He strapped himself in while, in the chair opposite, William Bertrand puffed on his pipe and, for the first time, blew an impossible plume of purple smoke into the air around them.

'Showtime,' he smiled.

And then the portal opened and, with a blinding flash of light, William and Herbert disappeared into the past.

CHAPTER EIGHT

Rough Landing

Herbert's eyes were fixed on the lights firing past the window, his hands wrapped tightly around the straps pulled over his shoulders. William was totally relaxed, puffing away on his pipe. The lights on the dashboard pulsed and blinked and were accompanied by a gentle beeping sound.

'You ready?' asked William.

Herbert peeled his eyes from the window. 'I don't know what to expect. So I'm not sure if I'm ready or not.'

William smiled and raised his pipe. 'You'll be fine.'

Herbert's ears were hissing and popping during the transfer, not unlike the feeling he'd experienced on holiday flights over the years. The machine was juddering and shaking more violently. Herbert could feel tiny beads of sweat trickling down his back. William sat with his head back, legs crossed and eyes closed, his pipe once again grasped between his teeth. He looked like he was enjoying a relaxing afternoon at home.

The lights on the dashboard became more intense and the *whap! whap!* sounded again.

'Here it comes!' said William, without opening his eyes.

The lights outside stopped, the rumbling ceased, and the time machine felt as if it had stopped moving under its own power and was simply floating.

Just as Herbert was wondering if they'd encountered a problem, the engines roared, the rumbling returned and the time machine came back to life.

'Well, we're through,' announced William, opening his eyes and smiling at Herbert.

The sounds on the dashboard continued, but the shaking had stopped. Outside, a faint orange hue emanating from the engines was the only blot of colour on the black canvas.

'Now, get those straps nice and tight,' warned William. 'Sometimes it can get a little bumpy when we land. When we walk out of here, I want you to know that no harm can come to us.'

'*Harm?*' asked Herbert, his voice cracking.

'Although,' William went on, extending his right hand upwards and rearranging his glasses so they sat perfectly on his nose, 'I must admit that I always forget that myself and end up ducking for cover, no matter how many times I come back here.'

'So we won't be in any danger?'

William shook his head. 'None.'

'And that's the case for every trip, is it?'

William winked at Herbert and tapped the side of his nose. 'Now, that would be telling.'

They juddered to the right, then shot into the air before dropping at pace, like a plane rolling around in the sky as it hit a patch of turbulence. Herbert gripped his straps harder.

'I told you it could get a bit bumpy,' shouted William.

The shaking increased, and for one minute it appeared they were going to crash to the ground. How could something so small withstand such a battering from the elements outside?

A faint alarm sounded from somewhere below them. Herbert flicked his head one way and the other, trying to find the location of the sound. Were they going to crash? And then he realised the sound of the alarm wasn't coming from the time machine itself, but from outside. It must be an air raid warning, thought Herbert, informing everyone to take cover. An attack from the German planes was imminent.

The beeping on the dashboard grew louder and a number of other lights were now flashing. Herbert sat watching as William unclipped himself, jumped from his seat and, with the pipe hanging out of his mouth, quickly pushed button after button.

'What's happening?' shouted Herbert, apprehension clear in his tone, but William was too busy adjusting dials to answer him. The beeping didn't subside but increased.

Herbert began to feel nauseous. He wasn't sure if it was because of the extreme movements, or because he was concerned they were about to crash. Saliva filled his mouth. He brought his hand up to wipe away the sweat forming on his brow and noticed William do likewise, only he used a handkerchief. Obviously, he wasn't as common as Herbert, who'd simply used the back of his hand!

'What do you want me to do?' asked Herbert, trying to unclip himself.

Without turning, William simply threw one hand behind him and pointed at Herbert. 'I want you to remain seated. I've got this!'

'Really?'

'Of course. I do it all the time. It's never quite this bad, though. Must be the additional weight!' he chuckled.

How can he make jokes at a time like this? thought Herbert and glanced out of the window. There was now a slight orangey-red glow, gently pulsing away. The sirens from outside had increased in volume and were soon joined by the faint sound of screaming from below ... they were getting closer.

William gave his brow another wipe before dropping into his seat and fumbling around with his straps. 'Here we go!'

Herbert was about to witness, first-hand, how appalling World War II was, and the devastation caused by the constant bombardment of the German planes.

The machine landed with a bump and a judder, the lights inside faded, and the beeping ceased. They'd arrived.

Herbert took a deep breath and brushed himself down, while William cleaned his pipe and placed it in the top-left pocket of his dustcoat.

'Ready?' asked William, standing up.

'I guess so,' replied Herbert, joining him in getting to his feet.

William wrapped his spindly fingers around the lever and pushed the door open.

A faint buzzing filled the sky as another Luftwaffe squadron approached, ready to bomb London once more.

CHAPTER NINE

World War II

Herbert stepped outside and couldn't believe the sight that greeted them. The hysterical screams of men, women and children mixed with the haunting sound of sirens that pierced the air. Some buildings remained, but others had been completely destroyed; there were huge piles of rubble everywhere. The bright orange glow of raging fires burnt all around. Red-hot ash floated blissfully towards the ground, while acrid black smoke billowed up into the sky. In the distance, the faint hum of another impending air attack was getting closer. Herbert stood, unblinking.

'Is there nothing we can do?'

'Like what?' asked William.

'We can't just stand here and watch,' pleaded Herbert. 'These people need our help or they're going to die!'

'Herbert ... We can do nothing. Besides, this is actual history you're watching unfold.'

'What?'

William used his pipe to indicate the panicking families running right past them. 'It's already happened ...'

'But there are children ... *young children*. There has to be something we can do!'

William lowered his pipe and solemnly shook his head. 'I know how you feel. It was the same for me, and I lived through the war as an adult. It isn't nice, but it gives you a different perspective on what everybody had to live through, don't you think?'

Herbert didn't answer. Instead, he turned and watched, powerless, his eyes frantically scanning the scene in front of him.

Eventually, he spotted a young woman struggling with a baby, about eighteen months old, hitched up on her hip. She was running and crying at the same time. The baby's mouth was open, and its face was bright red. Seconds later, the scream building up from deep inside its tiny chest, exploded. The lady raised one hand and stroked the baby's cheek, trying to calm it, while giving the occasional glance behind to encourage two other children – Herbert guessed were between five and seven years old – to hurry along. People were running right past the struggling family, not offering any help, in their desperate rush to reach the air raid shelter.

'To hell with this!' Herbert shouted and bolted towards the woman. 'Here, let me help you.'

The woman couldn't have heard him over the pandemonium. She didn't even look his way. More and more people ran past, trying to escape the attack.

Herbert bent down, opened his arms as wide as he could, and wrapped them around the boys. His first thought was how incredibly light they were.

'I've got you,' he whispered.

But then Herbert looked down and that's when he realised why they were so light: his arms were empty. *He didn't have them.*

He came to a stop in the middle of the rubble-strewn road and spun around. The woman was still there, running with the screaming child jiggling on her hip, and the two boys, whom Herbert had tried to gather up, following close behind. Tracks of their tears and soot from the battle coated their frightened faces. Herbert felt his own heart break.

There would be thousands of children like this all over London, and he could do nothing to help any of them.

More and more people rushed past. The woman and her three children were soon swallowed up by the crowd and disappeared. Herbert looked towards William, who was sitting on the rubble in front of the time machine. He shrugged and shook his head. Herbert trudged back over to him, shoulders hunched.

'We can't help, can we?' he asked, the words leaving a bitter taste in his mouth.

William shook his head.

'Then why bring me here?'

'Because you wanted to come,' replied William. 'If you didn't, you wouldn't have followed me to the basement, would you? We've changed nothing here, Herbie. We're simply watching events that have already happened, observing history from a front-row seat, if you will. We're not in a position to make changes to historical events – and even if we were, who's to say what's best in the long run? We might make changes that seem good now, but they might have a detrimental effect in the future ... No, the past is the past, Herbie, and it will forever remain so.'

In the distance, explosion after explosion sounded and the crumbling of buildings rumbled through the smoke-filled sky. Herbert's heart ached with the realisation that, given the state of the buildings all around them, people must have been through this many times already. They were only ever one attack away from losing their lives.

The sky above them filled with German bombers as they flew past, having made their latest devastating drop.

Herbert looked up. There were so many of them, these people didn't stand a chance.

Once the planes had passed, Herbert sat down next to William, folded his arms and braced them across his knees. The fires, the smoke, the burnt-out buildings, and the people – *most notably the children* – how would they ever recover?

His shoulders slumped and he rested his head on his forearms. 'How did we ever get out of this mess? How did we win?'

'How do you think we got out of this mess, Herbie?'

Herbert turned his furrowed brow towards William, but no words came.

William rested his withered hand on Herbert's shoulder. 'Because we're British, and it's what we do. Stiff upper lip and all that,' he said, sounding proud, then added, 'Right, I think it's time we got back home.'

William eased himself to his feet, closely followed by Herbert, who took one final look around, wiped his eyes and entered the time machine, closing the door behind him.

In the background came the sound of another aerial assault as the Luftwaffe planes approached once more.

They were soon soaring through the sky, on their way back home. Herbert could still hear the cries of the people, still smell the smoke and feel the intense heat of the fires. His arms still ached with the emptiness of the two boys he'd desperately wanted to save. He tried to forget them, but he was finding it difficult.

'So, what's this all been about?' asked Herbert after some time.

'What do you mean?'

'I have a feeling there's a reason you approached me in your museum.'

William looked intently at Herbert with his wise old eyes as the smoke from his pipe – not purple this time, but red – circled his head. 'Well, you were showing an interest in the war artefacts, so I thought it might be nice to show you a first-hand account.'

Herbert leant forward and looked directly into William's eyes. The museum manager shifted about in his seat. For the first time since the two had met, he looked unsure of himself, his eyes darting around nervously.

'Codswallop,' said Herbert. 'That's not the real reason.'

William took the pipe from his mouth, cleared his throat, and sat up straight. 'Okay, fine ... I need someone to look after this for a while. I have to go away on business and I need to leave it with someone I can trust. With your background, I thought you'd be the perfect candidate. I can't just leave it to anybody.'

'And how do you suggest I look after it? Gotta feed it twice a day or something have I?' joked Herbert.

'Don't be silly,' replied William. 'Although you do have some regular maintenance checks to make, they're no different to what you'd carry out on your car. It just means, instead of breaking down on the side of the road, you'll fall out the sky.'

'You're really selling this little project to me ...' said Herbert.

'Are you interested or not? You can have full use of it. Travel to anywhere in the past you want. Just like we've done ... It's so easy to use that I think even you could manage it.'

'Charming,' said Herbert. 'How long will you be away?'

'About a month, I'd say. But don't worry,' William added, 'I can shrink it down. It doesn't need to be quite this big.'

Herbert thought about it. He would have to keep Jean away from the garage, but it was only for one month. It shouldn't be too difficult. He could hide it at the back. Nobody would ever know.

Eventually, Herbert stood up, wiped the palm of his right hand on the front of his trousers and extended it to William. 'It's a deal. But only for a month.'

William stood and took Herbert's hand in both of his, shaking it vigorously. 'Yes, yes, yes, of course! One month. Thank you so much. This is such a huge relief, knowing someone like you will be looking after it.'

For the rest of the journey, William showed Herbert how everything worked. He told him places he should visit and more importantly, those to avoid.

Herbert was like a kid at Christmas. This was so exciting. He started thinking about all the places he could visit. The things he could do. And then a thought came to him, and the biggest smile broke out over his face.

'What is it?' asked William, noticing the smile.

'I've just had a thought ...' Herbert said, rubbing his hands together. 'I could go back. Try to find that lady with the three young children. See if they survived the war.'

William shook his head.

'What do you think?' asked Herbert. 'Would it be possible?'

'Herbert, you don't need to go back,' answered William, tapping his pipe on the armrest and taking another puff – the smoke had now changed to brightest gold.

'What do you mean?'

William removed the pipe and leant forward. 'She made it. She survived and so did the children. They lived a happy and peaceful life. In fact, they're still alive.'

'*Still alive*? All of them?'

'Yes.'

The smile on Herbert's face stretched almost as wide as the time machine itself. The young family had made it out of the war and lived perfectly normal, happy lives.

'So, you went back and checked on them?'

William shook his head, tapped his pipe, and popped it back in his mouth, inhaling once more. 'No.'

'Well, how do you know?'

William blew out a lungful of green smoke and winked. 'Because, Herbert, you were the one on her hip. That lady was your mum.'

CHAPTER TEN

Herbert's Surprise

Herbert and William arrived home safely. The return journey had been, thankfully, far less eventful. Herbert had remained strapped in his seat for the duration this time, ensuring there was no danger of him being sucked outside and hurtled towards the ground should the door fly open. He was struggling to believe he'd travelled back in time and seen his mum and his brothers, but he realised that was why William had taken him back to that precise moment. He'd wanted Herbert to see it, to form an emotional connection with the time machine and agree to take it for a month. He knew Herbert would want to go back and see his mum again. It had been a brilliant, though manipulative, plan.

'Here we are. Safe and sound,' said William after powering down the machine.

Herbert was closely followed outside by William, who put his pipe away and, once again, straightened his well-groomed hair.

'Told you we wouldn't get into any trouble,' he said, nodding at the large gold clock, which was displaying the same time as when they had left.

'Now, Herbie, are you sure you want to go through with this? It really would mean a lot to me.'

'Of course,' replied Herbert. 'Although, I do have one question.'

'What's that?'

'How am I meant to transport this to my garage? I mean, surely you can't make it small enough for me to simply slip it in my pocket?'

William winked and tapped the side of his nose. 'Leave it to me. I'll make the necessary arrangements. You won't have to lift a finger, I promise. All you have to do is nip down to your garage in the morning and make sure everything is alright.'

'Hold on ... You're moving it tonight?' asked Herbert.

'But of course! I leave in two days, and I've still a lot to organise. I have to make sure my cat is settled in with Mrs Liverbottom, then I have to contact

Agnes; she'll be looking after my house and collecting my post. After that–'

'Okay, okay, I get it,' interrupted Herbert. 'You have a lot to do. I don't need your complete itinerary. Make sure it goes right at the back.'

'Don't you worry,' said William, offering his hand. 'I'll make sure it's in the corner at the back.'

Herbert shook on it and made his way up the stairs, saying over his shoulder, 'See you in a month …'

'If not sooner!' William shouted after him.

When he reached the top step, Herbert eased the door open a crack to make sure nobody was around, pushed it open all the way, then stepped over the metal chain hanging loosely across the doorway. He cast his eyes around and hoped that he hadn't been spotted. The last thing he needed was someone wanting to see where he'd come from.

He made his way back to the World War II display and continued studying the artefacts. He was too young to remember much about the war, but one thing he could remember were the jubilant celebrations when it was all over.

His thoughts were interrupted as the school children came rushing over and Jasmine wrapped her arms around his waist.

'What's this, Daddy?' she asked, looking at the artefacts.

'This is the World War II display, princess.'

'Wow, look at all of that damage! It must have been a very scary time,' she said, pointing towards photographs of the devastating scenes. 'I'm glad I didn't live back then. I would have been worried all the time. We're much safer now, aren't we?'

Herbert looked into the innocent hazel-green eyes of his daughter, smiled and stroked her long blonde hair. 'We're much safer now. It was very scary back then, but not anymore. We won and we're all safe. There's no need for you to worry.'

He bent down and kissed the top of her head.

'Do you remember the war, Daddy?'

'A little bit. I was only young when it happened. But I remember a few things.'

'Maybe you can tell me sometime?' she asked. 'But only the nice bits. I don't want it to make me sad. I wouldn't like that.'

'I promise. Nothing but happy stories.'

'Look what I've got,' she said, holding up an activity book with both hands.

'Wow, a dinosaur book! Looks amazing, princess. You can tell me all about it when we get home.'

'I will. I like the T-Rex best, but he was really scary. It's a good job he had big teeth though, because he wouldn't have hurt you otherwise, not with such small arms.'

Herbert laughed. 'No good for doing this I bet.'

He bent down and tickled Jasmine until she cried with laughter.

'Daddy, stop!' she said, wriggling free. 'Look, we have to go now; everyone's leaving.'

Herbert looked up to see the school children making their way towards the exit. He was being beckoned to join them by the class teacher. He nodded and let go of his daughter, who ran over to join her friends. Herbert looked around to make sure none of the children were left behind and headed towards the exit to join the others boarding the coach.

Before going outside, he wanted to say goodbye to William. He stopped at the customer service desk to speak to the receptionist standing there.

'Hello, sir. Did you enjoy your visit?' she asked.

'Very much so,' Herbert smiled. 'But I was wondering – would it be possible to speak to Mr Bertrand? I'd like to thank him on behalf of the school.'

The receptionist's eyes darted around, and she began to fidget with a pen on the counter. 'Sorry, sir, I think I misheard you. Who did you want to see?'

'William Bertrand, the museum manager? Funny little man, walks around in an old dustcoat, wears a bow tie and smokes a strange pipe,' Herbert joked, before whispering, 'I also think his hair is painted on.'

The receptionist didn't smile or respond. Something was definitely not right.

'Well, is he ... around?'

'I'm sorry, sir,' the receptionist said, closing her eyes as they started to fill with tears.

'If he's busy I can come back again. It's fine,' Herbert offered, sensing there was a problem and not wanting to upset the young lady any more than he already had.

'He's not busy, sir ...'

'Oh, has he left already?' asked Herbert, realising how much William said he had to organise before going away the following day.

The receptionist raised a hand to cover her face. 'Please ... excuse me, sir.'

Without saying another word, she turned and hurried towards the toilet.

What was that all about? Herbert thought. Oh, well. He would see William when he got back in a month, anyway, so it was no problem. Although, he couldn't help but wonder why the young lady was so upset. Had something happened to William since they parted, just a few minutes ago?

Herbert's eyes wandered back to where the basement doorway had been – and his blood ran cold. There was a bronze statue of someone wearing a long dustcoat, thick-rimmed glasses, and a bow tie. His hair looked well-groomed, even on the statue, and a pipe was raised to his smiling lips.

Herbert walked over to get a closer look, his heart beating faster with every measured step. He stopped in front of the statue and read the gold plaque beneath.

'In loving memory of our founder, William Bertrand, 1905 - 1980.'

Herbert froze. How could this be? William was dead and had been for two years? To add to the mystery, the commemorative statue was positioned in a corner of the museum where previously there'd been a doorway with a chain hanging loosely across it, denying entry.

The entrance to the basement was gone.

2008

CHAPTER ELEVEN

30th of July 1966

After hearing all about the museum manager, Jack knew what the figures on the digital display signified: 30:07:66 was a date. He had no idea what event the date marked, but he was certain it would be something very exciting. The possibilities were endless – and there was only one way he was going to find out.

'What's that date, Grandad?' asked Jack, pointing at the digital display.

'What do you mean, *what's that date*? It's only one of the most famous dates in British sporting history: the 1966 World Cup final!'

Herbert explained all about the world cup and why it was so historic, but he didn't let Jack know the result of the final. This was going to be such an experience for him, and not knowing the outcome made it even more special, for Herbert as well as Jack.

They landed and made their way outside. Jack stood, eyes wide, taking in the sight of Wembley Stadium. It looked so different to the magnificent arena that Jack was used to seeing on TV.

'What do you think, Jack?' asked Herbert.

Jack continued staring at the old-fashioned stadium. 'This is Wembley?'

'This is what Wembley used to look like. What do you think?'

There was no arch stretching from one end to the other. No statue of Bobby Moore standing proud with his left foot placed on top of the ball, arms folded across his chest. And there was no sign of the gleaming wall of windows, or state-of-the-art screens showing the latest news and information of upcoming events. No. This was a time before then, when the most distinguishing feature of the old stadium was its famous 'Twin Towers'.

'It looks so different.'

'Well, it is different, Jack. But one thing hasn't changed.'

'What's that?' asked Jack, his eyes finally settling on his grandad.

Herbert smiled, 'The excitement! Let's go!'

Jack and his dad had watched matches on TV over the years, and had even been to watch Plymouth Argyle on several occasions, but being here, now, it was so different. Men, women and children were jumping around, shouting, and hugging each other. Their thoughts filled with the possibilities of what the day might bring. There weren't hundreds of replica shirts emblazoned with the names and numbers of players you see at every ground these days. Jack began to realise that perhaps that trend hadn't started yet. But what was the same was the buzz, the excitement and the nervous tension flowing through every supporter. Jack watched them all, in awe, as they moved towards the stadium like a big tidal wave, chanting, singing, and telling people they didn't even know that 'the boys' were going to do it. Chants of 'Eng-er-laaand, En-ger-laaand,' filled the air, along with the sound of wooden ratchets being enthusiastically spun around. The ear-piercing shrill of whistles and horns being blasted, added to the atmosphere. England hats, jackets, rosettes, and scarves were everywhere. The whole area was awash with expectant fans. Children were on their parents' shoulders, waving at anyone who paid them attention.

Jack turned to look at his grandad, who was standing next to him, tears of pride in his eyes.

As they made their way into the stadium, apprehension coursed through Jack's veins. They walked through the turnstiles, climbed the steps, and the noise exploded all around them, filling Jack's ears. They made their way past the crowds towards the luscious green grass of the stadium's turf. Jack's hands went to his mouth, covering the smile stretching across his face.

'Not bad, eh?' said grandad. 'Come on, keep moving, Jack, all the way to the front.'

The crowd were getting restless. Nervous energy was pouring out of everyone. And then a crescendo of noise rumbled through the stadium. The expectation was building, and the hairs on the back of Jack's neck stood to attention. Flags and scarves were being waved frantically as the officials walked out of the tunnel to a cacophony of noise, followed by the teams. West Germany wore crisp white shirts, black shorts and white socks, while England wore bright red shirts, white shorts and matching red socks. They were led out by their 'Captain Fantastic', Bobby Moore, the orange ball resting, as it always did, on his left hip. He looked so relaxed, like he was doing nothing more than going out for a Sunday morning stroll, not leading his country into battle with the old enemy for the most prestigious trophy in world football.

Herbert led them past the front row and towards the white fence separating the pitch from the crowd. Jack was waiting for somebody to come and tell them off, but nobody came. Suddenly, Jack realised why: he and his grandad were invisible. His heart was beating so fast, his palms were sweating, and he couldn't hear a thing over the noise. The atmosphere was electrifying. He couldn't wait for the game to start.

On the pitch, the referee gave one shrill blast of his whistle and the game was underway. It would prove to be a nail-biting match from the very first minute. Jack watched every kick, header, foul and tackle. It was gripping.

With the scores tied at 1–1, England thought they had won when Martin Peters swept the ball home to give England a 2–1 lead with only twelve minutes remaining. They were going to do it! But in the final minute, with the England fans already celebrating in anticipation of becoming world champions, West Germany won a free kick ten yards outside the England penalty area. The ball was driven into the area and ricocheted around before disaster struck: it was bundled home with almost the final kick, levelling the scores at 2–2 and taking the game into extra-time. Jack dropped his head in his hands. The German fans were in a euphoric mood, as if they had won the final. But they hadn't. Not yet.

England looked down and out, but after one hundred minutes of pulsating football Geoff Hurst scored the most controversial goal in world cup history. The ball crashed against the crossbar and thumped back down again before being headed over for a corner. However, the linesman deemed the ball had crossed the line and the goal was given, much to the elation of the England players and anger of the West Germans, who had surrounded the referee. But it was no use. The goal stood. It was 3–2. England were back in front. Surely they would hang on this time? But with the game entering the final minute, there was still time for more drama.

The ball was floated into England's penalty area, making Jack bring his hands up to his face and watch the action through splayed fingers. West Germany were pushing for another late equaliser, but Bobby Moore, looking as pristine and elegant as he had when he walked out of the tunnel before the game, casually brought the ball down on his chest.

'Kick it away! Kick it away!' yelled Jack.

But England's captain didn't kick it away. Instead, he played a one-two with a teammate before nonchalantly striding forwards with the ball.

'Grandad, why doesn't he just kick it away?' shouted Jack, bouncing up and down. 'It's nearly over!'

England's number six was the only person in the stadium not panicking. He looked up and effortlessly sent a fifty-yard pass upfield. Some people were running onto the pitch; they must have thought it was all over, but it wasn't. Not yet. Geoff Hurst collected the ball and drove towards West Germany's goal. Jack was bouncing up and down even more enthusiastically, and screaming with excitement. England's centre forward entered the penalty area and sent the ball flying unerringly into the top corner to complete his hat-trick. With the score at 4-2 and only seconds remaining, there was no way back for West Germany. It was all over. England had done it.

The crowd erupted into euphoric celebrations; ratchets were twirled; men, women and children were all hugging and jumping over each other. It didn't matter if they knew each other or not: England were World Cup Champions. Strangers hugged each other, men were crying, women were crying – even children were crying.

Eventually, Bobby Moore led his team up to Her Majesty the Queen and received the trophy.

As the winning team paraded around the pitch, their magnificent leader was hoisted onto his teammates' shoulders, holding aloft the sparkling Jules Rimet trophy.

Some time later, the crowds poured out of the stadium, delirious with the triumph, singing and dancing their way home. England supporters were everywhere: red, white, and blue stretched as far as the eye could see. Three young men, all wearing hats and scarves, stumbled by with their arms linked around each other and began singing and laughing. 'Two world wars and one world cup, doo-dah, doo-dah ... Two world wars and one world cup, doo-dah, doo-dah ...'

Everyone around them cheered and slapped their backs as they ambled by. Only twenty-one years after the devastating events of World War II, it was obvious this was more than just a football match, no matter how important it was.

Jack turned around and was shocked to see his grandad singing along with them. He winked at Jack and began wiggling his hips as he fist-pumped the air. People were running past, laughing and smiling, as they looked ahead to a night of celebrations. In the distance, fireworks exploded in the sky, lighting it with reds, blues, silvers, and golds. The supporters shouted their approval and the singing reached a crescendo as more and more ecstatic fans swarmed together.

'Did you enjoy that, my boy?' asked Herbert.

Jack nodded his approval. 'It was awesome, Grandad!'

'See. I told you there was nothing to be scared of,' said Herbert, ruffling Jack's hair.

And with that, they climbed the steps and headed home.

On their way back, Herbert told Jack all about the time machine and what they could do and where they could go.

'You mean we can visit anywhere, Grandad?'

Herbert nodded. 'Wherever you want. We can watch more famous football matches, see historical events, such as when the pyramids were built, or even meet world leaders. Any moment in history you want to see, we can. How does that sound?'

Jack beamed, 'It sounds amazing.'

He couldn't stop smiling the whole way back. His head was filled with the endless adventures he could have with his grandad.

If only Jack knew what the future held.

2012

CHAPTER TWELVE

Grandad Calls

Jack was straight out of bed at 8 o'clock, as soon as his alarm sounded. It may well be Saturday, meaning there was no school but, unlike other children his age, Jack had no interest in lying in bed until lunchtime. This wasn't because his mum and dad had something exciting planned, but because it was the day he would be off on another adventure with his grandad.

He pulled on his dressing gown and slippers and headed downstairs into the kitchen, where he was met with the unsavoury sight of his dad's bottom stuck up in the air as he dug around in the cupboard underneath the sink. A pile of tools lay next to him. Jack could hear his muffled expletives while the sound of banging made it clear something was broken and his dad, who was the worst person in the world at DIY, was attempting to fix it himself, rather than call in a professional.

'You okay, Dad?' asked Jack, reaching up and removing a glass from the cupboard above the sink.

'Oh, yes, Jack! I'm on top of the world. Can't you tell?' The sarcasm was unmistakable. 'I mean, I yearn for this every Saturday. I wish more things could go wrong in this poxy house!'

Jack rolled his eyes and turned on the tap to let it run cold before filling his glass.

'Aagghh!' cried Pete Mitchell, backing himself out of the cupboard and banging his head in the process. Jack turned off the tap and stepped away from the sink, empty glass in hand.

His dad clambered to his feet, water dripping from his face. 'What did you do that for?'

'Sorry, Dad. I didn't know what you were doing down there.'

'Oh dear, what happened Pete?' asked Jack's mum. She walked over, placed two hands on her son's shoulders and kissed the top of his head. 'Morning, sweetie.'

'He—' replied Jack's dad, pointing at his son with the spanner clenched tightly in his right hand, '—

thought it would be clever to turn the tap on while I was fixing the leak!'

'Well, did he know you were attempting to fix the leak?' asked Jasmine.

'Seriously?' moaned Pete, motioning towards the tools lying at his feet.

'Did you tell him, or just assume he'd know?'

'Well, no, but–'

'Well, there you go then!' Jack's mum shook her head and walked across the kitchen to the kettle. She switched it on before turning back to face the scene.

Pete wrung out his wet t-shirt and moaned, 'I'm soaking. I mean, seriously, look at me, Jaz.'

'Oh, I do, my darling. Every single day,' joked Jack's mum before turning back to her son. 'Go and have your cereal. There's juice on the table, too. I'm going to phone a plumber.'

'We don't need a plumber. I can do this,' whined a very disgruntled Pete.

Jasmine turned to see the sorry sight of her husband, standing with the spanner still hanging from his hand, and smirked. 'I think it's best we get someone in who knows what they're doing before we end up floating down the street.'

Smiling, she aimed a wink at Jack before heading towards the phone. But as Jasmine reached for the handset, it began to ring.

'Oh, I wonder who that could be?' she smiled, looking directly at her son.

'Hello? Oh, hi, Dad, how are you?' she asked. 'Yes, he's just having breakfast ... Well, can't it wait? ... Ok, fine.' Jack's mum sighed. 'I'll get him for you. Oh, I'm fine by the way ... thanks for asking ...'

Jasmine rolled her eyes and held the phone out to Jack. 'It's your grandad.'

Jack rose from the table, rushed over and put the phone to his ear, eager to find out what his grandad had planned. 'Hello?'

'Tell him he has a daughter who wouldn't mind a meaningful conversation now and again,' added Jack's mum, shaking her head as she walked away.

'Jack, my boy!'

'Hi, Grandad. Why don't you phone me on my mobile?'

'Well, you might think it's your grandma calling and not answer. I know I wouldn't!'

'No, Grandad,' said Jack. 'You've got different numbers, so I'll know who's calling me. I've told you that so many times, but you never listen.' Jack started to giggle. 'And just so you know, I'll always answer the phone to grandma. It's you I'd ignore!'

'Charming! Well, you know me and technology, I'm blinkin' useless ...'

Jack could imagine him waving a dismissive hand. 'Mum says hi by the way.'

'Yeah, I just spoke to her ...'

'I think she was being sarcastic because you ignored her when she answered.'

'Women!' tutted Herbert. 'Anyway, never mind that. Your grandma's heading off out with Eccentric Ethel today, so, do you wanna pop over?'

Jack could hear his grandad chuckling to himself.

'Of course,' replied Jack. 'Why are you so excited?'

'You'll find out when you get here. I've got a little surprise for you ...'

'Okay.'

'Well, gotta go, I can hear the sloth approaching.'

And with that, the line went dead.

'Wait! ... Well, bye then, Grandad,' mumbled Jack, pulling the handset away from his ear and staring at it as if he expected his grandad to phone back.

What crazy adventure did he have in store this time, Jack wondered, as he made his way upstairs to get ready.

After dressing in his newest jeans and favourite t-shirt, he wrestled his red hoody with the white draw strings from his wardrobe and headed back downstairs, pulling it over his head as he entered the kitchen.

His mum was sitting at the table drinking a cup of tea and leafing through the newspaper. Jack was more like her than his dad. They had the same blonde hair, identical hazel-green eyes, and the same slender build. He was all his mum's son, not at all like the slightly rotund, balding person that was his dad – who, incidentally, was nowhere to be seen.

'Where's dad?'

Jack's mum turned. 'Gone for a shower.'

Jack laughed. 'Another one?'

She gave Jack the warmest smile, which, years ago, must have captured the heart of his dad.

'Did you do it on purpose?' she asked.

'I promise, Mum, I didn't!'

'Well,' she added, finishing the last of her tea, 'if it was me, I would have turned both taps on.'

Jack giggled and went to grab his blue Nike trainers from the shoe rack.

'Where're you off to? Or do I really need to ask?'

'Gonna pop over and see grandad for a bit.'

'Now, why does that not surprise me? He's not teaching you anything he shouldn't, or getting you into anything dangerous, is he?'

'No ... We're just messing about in his garage, making stuff. That's all. It's good fun. You should come and look sometime.'

'Are you kidding?' she asked, her nose wrinkling. 'You wouldn't catch me or your grandma in that smelly mess of a garage.'

Jack pointed at the clock above the cooker, which told him it was already nine-twenty. 'Well, I gotta shoot. I told grandad I'd be there by ten.'

'You need a lift?'

'No, it's okay. I wanna go on my bike. Don't worry, I'll be careful,' he added, cutting her off before she could issue her usual plea for him to be careful.

'Okay, well I'm off to meet the girls in a bit. You take care,' she said, kissing the top of Jack's head a second time and putting her cup in the sink. 'And don't let your grandad get you into any trouble!'

As his mum disappeared upstairs, Jack smiled. 'I'm counting on it,' he mumbled to himself.

Jack lifted his coat from the hook and headed outside. He wondered what adventure they would be going on today. Their trips so far had been nothing short of amazing, but his grandad wasn't getting any younger. Herbert tried to hide it from Jack, but his grandson wasn't blind. He could see his grandad gripping the time machine and wincing as he descended the steps. It was something Jack didn't like to think about, but he had to. He knew these trips would have to end soon, and so he wanted to make the most of them while his grandad still could. Over the years they'd witnessed some of the most iconic moments in history, including the Battle of Hastings, in 1066, where King Harold was killed when an arrow pierced his eye. They'd also visited the seven wonders of the world, Jack's favourite being Petra in Jordan, because he loved the Indiana Jones films.

But today they would not be seeing any famous landmarks or visiting any historical events. They wouldn't be travelling back to 1901 and accompanying Captain Robert Scott on his Antarctic expedition. They wouldn't find themselves hiding in amongst the bushes, with a young David Attenborough, spying on some of the most magnificent creatures to ever roam the earth, and they wouldn't be standing on the deck of a slowly submerging RMS Titanic on its maiden voyage from Southampton to New York. No, today would be nothing like that. What Herbert had planned for them was about to change Jack's entire life.

CHAPTER THIRTEEN

Herbert Remembers

On the other side of town, Herbert had showered and dressed in his best casual clothes of beige chinos, blue boat shoes and a blue-and-white checked shirt. His outfit was finished with a brown cardigan thrown over the top. He was squinting and checking himself out in the mirror when Jean walked in, her arms full of clean laundry.

'For God's sake, Herbert. Will you please go and get your eyes tested?'

Herbert huffed. 'What do I want to do that for?'

'Because, you stupid man, they will prescribe you glasses!'

'Really?'

'Yes.'

'And then I'll see things clearer, will I?'

'Yes, of course. Everything will become crystal clear.'

'Even you?'

'Yes!'

Herbert sniggered. 'In that case, no thanks, Jean. I think I'll pass!'

Jean tutted, finished putting the laundry away and turned to her husband. 'Anyway, why are you dressed all snazzy?'

'*Snazzy*? Are we back in the nineteen-thirties?'

'Oh, don't be silly. You got another woman?' she asked, looking him up and down, her hands resting on her hips.

'Of course I haven't,' replied Herbert, shaking his head.

'Oh, shame,' she said, turning and leaving. 'I would have helped you pack!'

Herbert pulled a funny face as she left.

He'd hardly slept the night before. Ever since Jack first discovered the time machine, this was the trip Herbert had been most excited about. But now the day was finally here, he was nervous. He only hoped that everything went to plan.

He made his way downstairs to prepare for the day ahead, only to be told by Jean that her friend, Ethel, was running late. Jean tried telling Herbert why she'd been held up, but he was far too busy giggling and drawing funny faces on all the eggs in the fridge to listen about Eccentric Ethel's problems.

He quickly closed the fridge door before Jean could catch him in the act. 'Well, what time is she going to be here? I thought you were going out at nine-thirty?'

'I don't know, do I?' answered Jean. 'Honestly, Herbie. Her neighbour's husband has just walked out on her ... Don't be so selfish.'

'Huh. Can you get him to call me and tell me how he did it?'

'Oh, don't be so silly ...' Jean tutted, before she turned and walked out of the kitchen.

Herbert checked his watch. It was a quarter past nine. Jack would be here shortly. He had no idea what his grandad did when he was younger – Herbert hadn't mentioned it – but Jack would not only find out today, he would experience it first-hand. Herbert's heart raced as he remembered the most amazing summer of his life; the cars, the people and the feeling of utter jubilation at what he'd achieved. A smile crept across his face. He would soon be back there, and this time he would be going with the most special person in his life: his grandson.

CHAPTER FOURTEEN

Childish Herbert

'Jack!' beamed Jean as she opened the door.

'Hi, Grandma.'

She wrapped her arms around him. 'Do you want something to eat?'

'No, thank you. I've just had breakfast.'

'Are you sure? I can make you some crumpets?'

'No thanks,' insisted Jack, removing his bike helmet and bag and hanging them on the hook in the porch with a sign above it that read: *Jack's Stuff*.

'I do wish you wouldn't ride that death-trap over here,' said Jean, forever fretting about Jack cycling the two miles to their house. 'I'm sure your mum would drop you off if you asked her.'

'Grandma, it's not a *death-trap* – and I use the cycle path most of the way, anyway. You don't have to worry about me anymore, I'm a big boy now,' said Jack, stepping into the front room.

It had looked the same for years. There was a glass cabinet that was a shrine to Jack. It contained various photographs of him: as a baby sitting on his grandad's knee with a bright red party hat on his head; his first school photo, where he was smiling proudly, even though he had no front teeth; and, finally, one of him being smothered by his grandma. There were numerous items he'd made over the years and, weirdly, a lock of his baby hair in a pot. He kept asking his grandma to remove it because it was creepy, but she was having none of it.

'That was from your very first haircut,' she said. 'It brings tears to my eyes just thinking about it.'

Hanging along the wall behind the cabinet were several pictures and more family photographs. In the corner, next to the window seat, was an old rocking chair, its thick wooden armrests curling into claws at the ends. On a stand in the opposite corner sat a record player, with his grandad's old vinyl records piled up on a shelf beneath it. A doorway at the far end led into the hallway and, beyond that, the kitchen.

Jack's grandma, who'd walked in behind him, wrapped her arms around his neck and pulled him in for a protective hug. 'I know you're a big boy now, but you're still my baby!'

'For God's sake, put the boy down, Jean,' said Herbert as he entered the room. 'His head's gonna pop off if you squeeze him any tighter!'

Jean released Jack and spun around to face her husband.

Jack stood laughing as his grandad raised his fists then bobbed and weaved from side to side, like a boxer.

'Stupid man,' muttered Jean, squeezing past him.

'Jean, there's no need to get so close when you walk past me,' joked Herbert, raising his hands. 'I know you find me irresistible, but we have company!'

'Oh do shut up, Herbie,' said Jean, as she headed off in the direction of the kitchen.

Herbert turned around, his eyes wide and his mouth formed into a tight circle, which caused Jack to laugh out loud.

'You're going to get into serious trouble one day, Grandad.'

Herbert waved a dismissive hand at his grandson. 'That happened years ago when I married her. Anyway, how are you doing, my boy?'

'I'm good thank you. I thought you said grandma was going out?'

Herbert rolled his eyes and turned to check his wife wasn't within earshot. 'Eccentric Ethel isn't here, yet. Been held up. Apparently, her neighbour's husband has left her. Probably fed up living next door to that old biddy. So, of course, Ethel wants to get the gossip first, which she'll be asked to keep to herself, but your grandma will know all about it before the end of the day.'

'Is she really that bad?'

'Put it this way ... imagine your grandma's grumpiness and multiply it by ten.' Herbert held out his open palms, fingers extended, as if Jack didn't understand what ten looked like.

'I like grandma,' Jack said, smiling. 'She's only ever grumpy with you, and I can see why ...'

Herbert placed his hands on his hips and frowned. 'I thought you and me were best friends? Not sure I like you anymore.'

'So, anyway, what's the plan for today?'

'Well, I–'

A knock at the door disturbed their conversation.

'Oh, God, here she is, the mega-dragon. Watch your eyes, Jack, she'll have them out before you can blink.'

Herbert sighed and headed into the porch to open the front door. 'Ethel, what an absolute delight it is to see you! How are you?'

The sarcasm made Jack cover his mouth to stifle a laugh.

'Herbert!' Ethel greeted him with a sneer. 'Is Jean in?'

'I'm afraid not,' answered Herbert. 'She's already left. If you hurry you might just catch her.'

Ethel tutted. 'I take it she's in the kitchen?'

'How's your neighbour doing?' Herbert asked, keeping Ethel on the doorstep and out of his house for as long as possible.

Jack rushed over to the chair in the corner so Ethel couldn't hear his sniggering.

Ethel sighed. 'She's in bits, bless her. I feel so sorry for her.'

'Yes, I can imagine ... Mind you, at least she's got you.'

'Yes, she has.'

Herbert continued. 'I mean, she's over there crying her eyes out because her husband's left her for a younger woman, and yet, here you are, waiting to go into town so you can tell my wife what a good friend you are for supporting your neighbour through this terribly dark time.'

Jack grabbed his ribs with one hand and covered his mouth with the other, making him slide off the chair and onto the floor.

'You're not funny, Herbert,' said Ethel, stepping inside. She frowned at the sight of Jack. 'What's up with him?'

'Oh, he's got fleas. Just rolling around to get a good itch. Shall I take your coat?'

Ethel winced and grabbed her large tweed coat around both lapels and brought it in closer to her chest. '*Fleas*? Where did he get them from?'

'Probably from school. Mind you, it's not as bad as last week ... he brought a rat home to dissect.'

'What!' yelled Ethel.

'Don't worry, we'll find the little tyke soon enough,' said Herbert. He closed the door and walked past her to pick up a broomstick leaning against the fireplace.

'What do you mean?'

'Well, Jack didn't want to kill it, so he let it go free. We ain't seen it since, but he's in here somewhere, the little bugger,' said Herbert, searching with narrowed eyes, the broomstick clenched tightly in both hands.

By now, Jack was in hysterics. He wasn't even trying to fight it anymore. His legs, raised in the air, looked like they were running the one hundred metre sprint, and his hands were slapping the carpet as he gasped for breath.

'Escaped?! Set free?!' cried Ethel, ignoring Jack. Her face, beneath a curly, blue-rinse hairdo, had turned pure white.

'Oh, it's fine. I heard him scratching earlier. Honestly, they're crafty little so-and-sos. I can't catch him.'

Ethel turned and marched towards the kitchen. Jack looked up just as Herbert brushed the broomstick gently across her ankle.

'Argh!' she screamed and ran through the door.

'Stupid woman,' smiled Herbert, before returning the broomstick.

'Grandad, you're terrible!' Jack spat out, wiping tears from his eyes.

Footsteps approached from the hallway. Jack and Herbert turned to see Jean and Ethel standing there with looks of utter disdain.

Jean's voice was more like a bark. 'Herbert, what have you done?'

'He was so mean to me,' explained Ethel, her hands clenched tightly around her handbag.

'Me? What did I do this time?' tutted Herbert. 'Honestly, you can't have a laugh these days.'

'You need to grow up,' Jean scowled. 'Be nice to my friends!'

Herbert raised his hands in a conceding manner. 'I apologise if I upset you, Ethel. I didn't mean to. It was just a joke …'

'Well, we're off,' huffed Jean. 'I'll be home in a few hours.' She brought the famous Finch finger up to Herbert's face and frowned at him. 'Behave yourself – and look after Jack.'

Jean pulled her coat off the hook and shrugged it on.

'Where are you going, anyway?' asked Herbert. Off to meet the other three?'

'What?' Jean snapped, clearly nearing the end of her tether with Herbert's immature behaviour.

'*The other three.* Are you off to meet them in town?'

'*Other three*? What *other three*?' asked a confused Jean, opening the door.

'Dear me,' said Herbert, shaking his head. 'The other Spice Girls! I'm guessing you're the sporty one,' he said, pointing at his wife, 'because of your … erm, athletic build. And you,' he said, turning to a sour-faced Ethel, 'must be that scary one, for obvious reasons.' Herbert tapped his chin and then raised a solitary finger as if he'd just remembered something important. 'Unless you're posh spice, because she always looks so miserable, too?'

Jack covered his mouth and sniggered.

The women merely tutted and headed for the open door.

'Oh, come on ladies!' said Herbert. 'It was just a joke. Don't get mad!'

Jean and Ethel ignored him.

'Okay, look. I'm sorry,' apologised Herbert, winking at Jack. 'I'll make it up to you.'

Ethel and Jean turned back to a smiling Herbert, who, barely able to contain his laughter, spluttered, 'Just tell me what you want ... what you really, really want!'

Jack was in fits of laughter, again. Hearing his grandad quote a line from the Spice Girls' first ever song was something he never expected.

'You really are a stupid man, Herbert Finch!' snapped Jean. 'Come on, Ethel, let's go.'

The women headed out of the door, slamming it shut behind them.

Herbert giggled and rubbed his hands together. 'Ready?'

'Ready ...' confirmed Jack, wiping yet more tears from his eyes.

Herbert clicked his fingers as if he'd forgotten something, picked up the broomstick and rushed to the front door.

Jack watched from the window seat, pulling the net curtain back for a clear view.

'Jean! Jean!' shouted Herbert, reaching the gate with the broomstick raised above his head. Jack's eyes were trained on his grandma and Ethel, who were stood across the street from them. He didn't want to miss their reaction.

'You forgot your car!' shouted Herbert, frantically waving the broomstick at the women.

'Oh shut up!' hissed Jean, turning and heading off in a strop.

Herbert came back into the house, giggling like a child and returned the broomstick. Jack could see the glint of excitement in his eyes.

'Let's go!' said Herbert, grabbing his newsboy cap from the sideboard.

Jack collected his bag and followed his grandad along the path towards the garage.

It was time for another adventure.

CHAPTER FIFTEEN

Jack's Nervous Grandad

The sun was climbing above the trees at the rear of the garden, shining brightly across the beautifully manicured lawn. The chirping of birds in the trees filled the sky, along with the faint hum of a siren in the distance. Water poured from the fountain jutting out from the fishpond, caressing the rocks before dropping into the water with a gentle *plink-plink*. The beautiful flowers lining both sides of the path were in full bloom with red, yellow, green, blue and purple petals. The sweet smell filled Jack's nostrils and were a total contrast to the aroma that would soon welcome him to his grandad's sanctuary: the garage.

Jack thought it was funny how his grandparents' prized areas of the house mirrored their own appearance. His grandma always smelt sweet and was meticulously clean and tidy, just like her garden. His grandad's garage was like the man himself: disorganised, smelly, and always looked like it had been neglected for years. But this morning Jack noticed his grandad had made a conscious effort to shower and dress in his finest gear. 'Saved for best' was how Herbert described it. He didn't even look this smart on the odd occasions he took Jean out. Jack wasn't sure, but he had a feeling the old man was up to something.

They reached the garage door and Herbert eased it open. The smell smacked Jack on the nose, as it did every week. He thought he'd be used to it by now, but no such luck. The bench was still full of pots of paint, pieces of wood, and old tools. Fresh wood shavings covered the floor, although there was never any evidence of any sort of woodwork being undertaken.

Herbert reached the rear of the old car and gave the faded lettering a double tap, like he always did. Jack had never seen his grandad do any work on the car and, with it taking up so much room, he wondered whether it would be better to simply scrap it. However, he knew his grandma hated it, so that was probably why his grandad had kept it all these years.

Herbert pulled the green sheet back and opened the door to the time machine. Before they stepped inside, he grabbed Jack by the shoulders and stared into his grandson's eyes. His normal cheeky expression had been replaced with something much sterner.

'Now, Jack, today's trip is a surprise. So, while I get ready for take-off, cover your eyes. I want this one to be extra special ...'

There was definitely something different about his grandad today. He looked nervous and had a peculiar smell about him. Was that aftershave? Jack wasn't even sure his grandad knew what deodorant was, let alone aftershave. But the smell of it felt a bit like dressing a tramp in a three-piece suit – weird.

'Grandad?'

'Yes?'

'What's going on?'

Jack's eyes narrowed as he watched his grandad's expression closely.

'What do you mean?'

'I mean, you're acting odd this morning.'

'It's nothing, Jack, honestly. I just want to get off for a bit of an adventure,' said Herbert with a forced smile.

Jack was having none of it. 'Fibber. I know there's something going on, but I'll do as you say – anything to get this weirdness over with. Maybe later you can tell me what this is all about?'

Herbert nodded. 'Excellent, that's the spirit. Now, in you get. All will be revealed soon enough, dear boy!'

They clambered in and Herbert secured the door before going about the normal pre-take-off routine. Jack settled into his seat and covered his eyes, as requested. Herbert shifted about, pushing buttons and twisting dials. The beeping of the alarm sounded and the engines began to rumble.

'Okay, Jack. You can look now.'

Jack lowered his hands. The digital display had been covered by a sheet.

'I told you, it's a surprise.'

Jack had his eyes firmly fixed on his grandad. He would normally be messing around, making funny faces, or telling jokes. But not today. Not this time. It was obvious this trip meant more to him than anything they'd done before.

Herbert couldn't settle; he began strumming his fingers on the armrests and his right foot was nervously tapping the floor. Then the rumbling exploded from beneath them and, as they descended underground, Herbert did something he'd never done before: he started biting his nails.

Jack had never seen his grandad like this. Dressed in his best attire, wearing aftershave, with his hair brushed (probably teeth, too, for that matter). He'd told Jack today was a surprise, but it was going to be far more than that.

But when they landed and stepped out of the time machine, everything would become clear. Jack would discover why his grandad was so anxious, and it would be for a reason he would never have expected in his wildest dreams.

CHAPTER SIXTEEN

How It All Began

Jack walked over to the window and watched as they gently drifted above the town below. He could hear Herbert huffing and puffing behind him, so turned to ask, 'Okay, what's going on? You've been on edge since we left. What's the big deal about today?'

'It's nothing, really. I'm just apprehensive because today's adventure means so much to me, that's all. There's nothing for you to worry about,' said Herbert, attempting a reassuring smile.

Jack smiled back, 'It can't be that bad – not after some of the places we've been. Remember when we went on that safari and ended up in the middle of a pride of lions?'

Herbert giggled, 'Yes, we did. Now, that was funny!'

'And you wanted to ride the biggest lion there.'

'Well, it was just a big cat really, wasn't it?'

Jack threw his hands in the air. 'Since when have you ever ridden a cat?'

'Never.'

'So why say it then?'

Herbert shrugged. 'Dunno. Thought it was funny.'

'So, what's the big deal with today? I've never seen you so nervous ...'

Herbert took a deep breath. 'Well, there's one place I've always wanted to take you. It's somewhere very close to my heart and means more to me than anything.'

'What, more than grandma?' Jack giggled.

Herbert didn't say a word but gave Jack a rueful smile. 'I want to take you back to the year that changed me and my life forever: 1962. I was twenty-four and had the world at my feet.'

Jack listened intently. He could tell he was about to get lost in another of his grandad's exciting stories.

'I was in my prime. Everyone knew it. I was, what you might say, the talk of the town.'

Jack didn't know if his grandad was pulling his leg, but he'd never seen him so focused on a story. He lowered himself back into his seat, ready to hear more.

'Well, although we're going back to 1962, the fun started ten years before that, when I was still in school,' said Herbert. 'It all began as a silly joke between four of us: me, Trevor Richardson, Brian Kilkenny and David Samuels. We were best mates, totally inseparable, and always looked out for each other. However, there was always one of us in trouble, which was usually me–'

'There's a surprise!' giggled Jack.

Herbert continued. 'One day we thought it would be a laugh to break into the science lab and steal some of the chemistry jars, mainly so we wouldn't have to take an exam the following day.'

'What!'

'I know, not the greatest idea, but we were young and foolish.'

'You're still foolish. Not sure about the young part, though.'

'Cheeky!' said Herbert, giggling and shaking his head. 'Anyway, the plan was to distract our teacher, Mr Stone – or Bony Stoney as we called him – and steal his keys to the equipment cupboard.'

'Why did you call him *Bony Stoney*?'

'Because he was six-feet-five inches tall and had long wiry arms and legs. He was so tall that he had to crouch down to write on the blackboard. He always looked like he was lowering himself onto the toilet!'

Jack giggled, which seemed to encourage Herbert all the more.

'And his face was so thin it looked like he'd squashed it in a vice. He was the most miserable man I've ever met! He always wore the same outfit to school: a tweed suit (complete with elbow patches), a brown shirt and a black bow tie. He reminded me of a stick insect.'

'So, what happened?' asked Jack, placing his elbows on his knees and using his palms to cradle his chin.

'It was a Wednesday night – the last Wednesday before we broke up for the summer holidays. It was a night I'll never forget. Nor would I forget the weeks that followed. It was the summer that completely changed my life, the summer of 1952.'

THE SUMMER OF
1952

CHAPTER SEVENTEEN

School Break-In

'Herbie, will you hurry up,' urged David.

'Calm down, Dave,' Herbert said, teetering along the curb twenty yards behind them. 'It's not like anybody's gonna see us. We're the only ones here.'

'Anybody could turn up,' added Trevor.

'Who?' asked Brian. 'Who's gonna come here at this time of night, Trev? Everyone rushes out of this prison at the end of the day – including the teachers,' he joked.

'I'm just saying we need to hurry, that's all. I mean, look at him,' said David, motioning towards Herbert, who had now left the curb and climbed onto a swing in the park opposite.

'Whee!' Herbert squealed, swinging higher and higher.

'Herbie!' snapped Trevor.

In one movement, Herbert let go of the swing and was momentarily airborne before landing on his feet and jogging over to his friends. 'Relax, Trev. You're getting old before your time, mate!'

David turned back to the fire exit door at the back of the sports hall, which had been left slightly ajar. He prised it open and stepped inside.

'Dark in here, innit?' remarked Brian.

'Dunno, can't see,' Herbert joked, making Brian snigger.

The door closed behind them and two lights pierced the darkness.

'I see the boy scouts have come prepared,' said Herbert, nudging Brian.

With a click, Brian's beam joined the others.

David turned to Herbert. 'I take it you didn't bring a torch?'

'No need, mate. I eat my carrots. I'm a good boy.'

Trevor led the way, sweeping his torch across the solid wooden floor as they headed towards the far end. Benches, stacked three high, were positioned along the wall on the left, with bags of various balls hanging above them. Climbing ropes attached to the ceiling were safely tucked away behind the horizontal monkey bars fixed to the wall on the right. A vaulting horse, with a pile of crash-mats on either side, stood at the back, beside the door that would give them access to the rest of the school building. The boys made their way past the equipment; the *tip-tapping* of their shoes the only sound in the otherwise empty sports hall.

'Anyway,' Herbert said, when they reached the far end, 'what's the plan?'

Trevor was getting annoyed. 'What do you mean, *what's the plan*? Were you not listening earlier?'

'Yeah. I was, but ...'

'*But what*?' Trevor snapped.

'I kind of forgot,' said Herbert with a shrug.

'Unbelievable,' said Trevor, shaking his head.

'Why is it always you?' asked David.

'Dunno. Just lucky I guess.'

Brian couldn't help it, he sniggered again. 'You're such an idiot, Herbie.'

'Why, thank you!'

David shook his head. 'Don't encourage him.'

'Come on,' said Trevor. 'We need to get to the science lab.'

'Right,' Herbert said, raising a finger, as if he understood, before adding, 'Why?'

Trevor replied, 'Because we're stealing the equipment of course.'

'Right ... but why?'

'Are you being serious?' asked David.

The boys paused by the door.

'So we don't have to take the end-of-year exam tomorrow that none of us have studied for,' explained Trevor.

'Got it,' said Herbert, with a simple nod of the head.

David opened the door, looked down the hallway and signalled that the coast was clear. They moved into the corridor and listened intently. Nothing, except an eerie silence – it was so strange being in the school after dark.

Herbert was first to speak. 'What are we nicking?'

'Oh, for goodness sake, Herbie!' David said, rubbing his forehead. 'You've not listened to anything, have you? You probably don't even know why me and Trev were fighting in class today.'

'Were you?' asked Herbert, sounding shocked at the revelation.

'Yes!'

'Oh, right ... Why was that, then?'

'What planet are you on, Herbie? Were you not listening when we planned it?'

'What do you mean?'

'Oh, never mind, just follow us,' said Brian.

The four teenagers crept down the hallway and headed towards the science lab. David led the way, his torch beam fixed down the centre, creating a spooky tunnel effect.

They spun around at the sound of tapping behind them.

'What was that?' asked Trevor, sweeping his torch in the direction of the noise. The beam landed on the culprit: a tiny mouse. It glanced in their direction before scurrying away and disappearing through the doorway that led to the sports hall.

'Maybe he's off to play a bit of football!' joked Herbert.

The group reached the end of the corridor, turned left and headed towards the door to the science classroom; the squeaking of its hinges magnified by the empty space. The four boys entered and made their way over to the equipment cupboard.

Herbert rattled the door. 'It's locked.'

Brian reached into his pocket and removed a set of keys. They jangled louder than any set of keys Herbert had ever heard. Brian located the correct key with shaking hands, inserted it, and unlocked the cupboard.

'How did you get hold of them?' asked Herbert, pointing at the keys.

Brian ignored him and pulled the doors open. The beams of the torches illuminated shelves full of beakers, test tubes and glass jugs.

David asked, 'How are we gonna do this?'

'Chuck them in this,' offered Herbert.

The others turned to see him holding up the classroom bin.

'What are you doing?' asked Trevor.

'We can use it as a container,' Herbert replied. 'Unless you have one up your jumper, Trev?'

'He's got a point,' Brian said, before quickly adding, 'for once.'

'I'll keep watch,' said David, and headed back over to the door.

'Yeah, good idea. That mouse might pop in here at any moment; we don't wanna get caught by the rodent police,' Herbert joked, placing the bin on the floor.

Brian and Trevor carefully emptied the items into the bin, taking care not to smash any.

'Okay, I think that's all we're going to fit in there,' said Brian. He locked the cupboard and stood up, before asking, 'Where's Herbie?'

'I'm over here,' came Herbert's voice from the other side of the teacher's desk.

Trevor and Brian trained their torches on Herbert, who was standing beside the blackboard.

Brian was about to lose his temper. 'What are you doing?'

'Leaving a message,' replied Herbert.

Brian read aloud, 'To Bony Stoney. Maybe you should take better care of your keys in future.'

Herbert explained, 'I know it's a bit messy, but I couldn't see. I don't have a torch.'

'You idiot! He's gonna know it was one of his class now!' said a panicked Trevor.

'He won't,' insisted Herbert. 'Stop stressing. Honestly, it's like being out with my grandparents!'

'Look, let's get out of here, we got what we came for,' Brian said. 'Herbie, you can carry the bin.'

'Yeah, let's go,' David agreed as he opened the door and led the four boys, with a school bin full of glass containers, back down the corridor.

'Glad the plan worked,' said Herbert.

'What do you mean?' David asked. 'You didn't have a clue what the plan was.'

Herbert shook his head in disagreement. 'Of course I did. You and Trev had a fight in class today to get Bony Stoney's attention away from his desk so that Brian could steal the cupboard keys from his drawer. We're going to dispose of these here,' he added, holding up the bin, 'because then we won't

149

have to take the practical chemistry exam tomorrow.'

The others stopped and turned their torches on Herbert.

'Easy, lads,' said Herbert, turning his head away from the bright beams.

'You mean you were listening?' asked an annoyed David.

'Of course I was,' answered Herbert. 'You know me. It's why you all love me so much. Why do you think Little Miss Goody-two-shoes squealed in class today?'

'You mean Charlotte Harris?' asked Trevor. 'I thought she was whining because we were fighting.'

Herbert shook his head. 'No, I tapped her on the shoulder and told her I saw something crawl under her collar. You know what a scaredy-cat she is. She was squealing and flapping at her hair while I flicked it with a ruler. I may have occasionally brushed it against her neck, too. It was so funny. Her hands were going wild, trying to get rid of the invisible pest!'

Brian asked, 'What did you do that for?'

'Because, you baboons, if there was one person who would've seen Brian and grassed him up, who would it have been?'

'Charlotte,' the others chorused.

'So I distracted her. She didn't see Brian, and we got away with it.'

'Why didn't you tell us?' asked David.

'What, and miss winding you lot up? Not bloomin' likely. Right, let's go,' said Herbert, and headed around the corner.

His friends looked at each other and shook their heads.

David said, 'He is unbelievable.'

'Funny though,' giggled Brian.

They rounded the corner and approached the open door of the sports hall; the gentle *clink-clink* of the containers joined the *tip-tapping* of shoes as they hurried towards it. They were eager to get outside and hide the containers before they were caught – not that there would be anyone around to catch them so long after school had finished. But, just as David wrapped his hand around the handle, it happened.

'Stop right there, all of you!' Mr Stone's booming voice echoed down the corridor.

'Go ...' Herbert whispered to his friends. 'I'll take care of this.'

David Samuels, Trevor Richardson and Brian Kilkenny wasted no time in bolting through the open doorway, leaving Herbert Finch to deal with the consequences of their break-in, all by himself.

The lights overhead buzzed, flickered, and eventually illuminated the corridor. Herbert, with his arms wrapped around the bin full of glass containers, waited for their wiry science teacher to reach him. The boys' prank had landed Herbert in big trouble, but it would also lead him on an unexpected journey to becoming the most dedicated student the school had ever seen.

CHAPTER EIGHTEEN

Herbert's Punishment

'Finch! Why am I not surprised it's you?'

Mr Stone marched towards Herbert and came to stop in front of him, hands on hips, while the footsteps of David, Trevor, and Brian faded in the distance.

'Wrong time, wrong place, sir.'

'Where are the others?'

'*Others*, sir?'

'You know who I mean. Samuels, Kilkenny and Richardson. You lot are always up to no good!'

'I have no idea what you're going on about, sir.'

'Don't give me that, Finch! I know they were here. I saw them go through there,' the teacher said, pointing towards the open door to the sports hall.

'Did you?' asked Herbert, turning and looking at the door.

'I know they were here, and I'm going to prove it!'

'Really? How, sir?'

'Don't get lippy with me, boy,' warned Mr Stone, grabbing Herbert by the collar. 'I know they were here, and so will the headmaster!'

'Blimey! He's working late.'

'You think you're so clever, Finch. Have an answer for everything, don't you?!'

'I wouldn't say *everything*, but–'

'That was a rhetorical question!'

Herbert knew he was landing himself in more trouble, but he couldn't help it.

'So, what do we have here?' asked Mr Stone, inspecting the bin. 'Oh, there's a surprise! Stealing school property. I'll have you expelled for this, Finch. You think I didn't know what you lot were up to today?'

'I don't know what you mean, sir.'

Mr Stone pushed his glasses up his long, thin nose and bent down so that he was inches from Herbert's face.

'Well, after class, when I couldn't find my keys, I knew you lot were up to something. The pathetic prank of fighting to distract me so that you could steal them may well have worked, if you weren't stupid enough to be running around and laughing together, during your lunch break. So, knowing how your little group operates, I just had to wait for you to show up tonight. With your exam set for tomorrow, this was your only opportunity to implement whatever childish prank you had planned.'

Mr Stone stood tall and puffed out his scrawny chest, adding, 'You see, Finch, I'm not as dumb as you lot. You needed to do better than that to outsmart me.'

Mr Stone smirked, looking very pleased with himself.

'Well, you're obviously not as dumb as you look, sir.'

'What did you say?'

Herbert remained silent.

'Well? Have you nothing funny to say for a change, Finch?' shouted the teacher. Spittle flew from his mouth, hitting Herbert in the face.

Herbert grimaced and closed one eye. 'Have you got a tissue, sir?'

'Oh, that's it ... You can explain yourself to the headmaster,' added Mr Stone. 'He's not going to be happy about coming in tonight, I can tell you that!'

He grabbed Herbert by the collar and marched him down the corridor.

The headmaster's office walls were covered with certificates and photographs from various school achievements over the years. Highly-polished sports shields and trophies glistened inside a glass display cabinet next to a window that overlooked the playground. The smell of lavender polish filled the room.

Despite being the school clown, Herbert was very rarely sent to the headmaster's office. He always made sure he stayed just on the right side of mischief. Not this time. Now he was in big trouble. He stared across a huge solid oak desk and into the storm-grey eyes of the headmaster, who was standing with his palms resting on its surface. Mr Hucklebuck cut an imposing figure. He was as tall as Mr Stone, but ever so much wider. His crisp white shirt struggled to contain his barrel chest and bulging arm muscles. He walked with a pronounced limp, but nobody dared ask him why. Herbert joked that he probably had a pebble stuck in his shoe. His closely shaven head made him look very intimidating, which meant bad behaviour in the school was at an all-time low. However, despite his thug-like appearance, Mr Hucklebuck had a calm and likeable personality, unlike the volatile Mr Stone.

'The police should be here with me, Finch. You do know that, don't you?'

'Yes, sir,' replied Herbert, sheepishly. He wasn't going to be as flippant with the headmaster as he had been with Mr Stone.

Mr Hucklebuck continued. 'Breaking and entering school grounds to steal school property, all because you don't want to take an exam: I should expel you on the spot.'

'Yes, sir.'

'He needs to be made an example of,' offered Mr Stone.

Mr Hucklebuck raised his hand, acknowledging his colleague's input, but his eyes remained fixed on the 14-year-old in front of him.

'And what about the others?'

Herbert frowned. '*Others*, sir?'

'Yes, Finch. Mr Stone said there were three other pupils with you.'

'I'm sorry, sir. I have no idea what you're going on about. I think Mr Stone needs to get his glasses checked. They appear to be faulty.'

Mr Stone's eyes nearly popped out of his head at Herbert's insolence. 'Don't lie, Finch. I saw them. They were involved in this, too!'

'Yes, thank you, Harold. I'll deal with this,' said Mr Hucklebuck, before turning back to Herbert. 'You're willing to take the punishment all by yourself, are you?'

Herbert's expression didn't change. His hands were clasped behind his back. The bin full of glass containers – evidence of his prank – had been placed on a chair to his right.

'Well, I am the only one here, sir.'

'Liar!' shouted Mr Stone.

'Thank you, Harold,' said the headmaster. 'Maybe it would be best if you waited outside ... unless you can confirm the identity of the others, of course?'

'We all know it was Samuels, Kilkenny and Richardson. It's obvious,' Mr Stone snapped. 'It's always those four. Always!'

'And you saw their faces, did you? Bear in mind that I cannot punish any student unless there's been a positive identification.'

'Well, I didn't see their faces, but I know it was them. Those four are as thick as thieves.'

'Did you see their faces?' Mr Hucklebuck repeated, eyebrows raised.

'Well, no. Bu–'

'Then I cannot punish them!'

'Of course you can–'

'Harold, please,' said Mr Hucklebuck, holding up his hand. He was clearly getting irritated with the science teacher's constant interruptions. 'Breaking into school, Finch. This is a new low. Even for you.'

Herbert remained silent. For such an imposing figure, the headmaster spoke in such a quiet and controlled manner it was worse than him shouting.

'Well?'

'*Well*, what, sir?'

'Why would you break into school to steal equipment and risk expulsion? Because that's where this is heading.'

Mr Stone couldn't help himself and muttered, 'About time, too.'

The headmaster had heard enough. 'Harold, kindly wait outside.'

'But, Mr Hucklebuck–'

'Now, Harold!'

Mr Stone turned and left, mumbling something under his breath.

Mr Hucklebuck walked around his desk and perched on the edge of it. 'Why, Herbert?'

Herbert shrugged.

'You've gone far beyond playing a little prank during school time. You've broken into school and taken property with the sole purpose of destroying it, just so you don't have to take an exam. It doesn't look good, does it?'

Herbert shook his head. 'I wasn't going to destroy them, sir, just hide them until next year. I've just not studied for chemistry, that's all ...'

'Well, maybe you should have thought about that sooner. Because, right now, you're in far more trouble than you would have been for failing the exam.'

'Huh! You should meet my parents.'

'The dilemma I'm faced with is that detentions do nothing to get to the root of the issue,' admitted the headmaster. 'You'll only brag about it and encourage others to do likewise, saying I'm an easy touch. I'm also not a fan of giving the cane: that does nothing to rectify ill-discipline, not to mention the fact I find that particular treatment barbaric. And we all know expulsion is not my favoured form of punishment: you would only get sent to another school and cause problems there, so all I'd be doing is passing the irresponsible, selfish, and disrespectful attitude you've displayed here on to another headmaster to deal with, which seems unfair. So, you can see the predicament I'm in.'

Herbert joked, 'Wouldn't wanna be in your shoes, sir.'

The headmaster was unimpressed. 'There's a time and a place for being funny, Finch. Now is not one of them.'

'Yes, sir,' said Herbert, dropping his gaze to the floor. 'Sorry, sir.'

'Therefore, I think a different form of punishment is required.'

Herbert looked up. '*Different*, sir?'

'Yes, Herbert. Now, as we are about to finish the school year, I have a proposition for you.'

'*Proposition*, sir?'

'I'm having some work done at my house. I have a small garage that needs to be cleared. Your punishment, should you prefer that over expulsion, would be to clean my garage out during the summer holidays. It should only take a couple of days, but it all depends how fast you work ...'

Herbert was confused. 'You want me to clean your garage, sir?'

'That's correct,' said Mr Hucklebuck, his shovel-like hands clasped in front of him. He looked like he could crush Herbert with very little effort.

Herbert was stunned. No detention, no expulsion and no having to explain to his parents what he'd been caught doing this time. It would be so easy to get away with. After all, it would only take a couple of days. His parents would never know. He could pretend he was out playing with his friends. It was perfect. Almost too perfect.

'What's the catch, sir?'

'*Catch*? There's no catch, Herbert. It's a punishment. Technically, you've committed this crime outside of school hours, so if you say no, that's fine. I'll call the police and you can get arrested for breaking and entering ...'

Mr Hucklebuck turned and picked up his phone. Herbert watched him dial the first two nines.

'Wait!'

The headmaster paused with his finger ready to complete the call. 'Yes?'

'I'll do it, sir. As long as my parents never find out.'

'I don't think you're in a position to make demands, Finch.'

'Please, sir. I'm going to be in big trouble if they do.'

Mr Hucklebuck lowered the phone back into its cradle and smiled. 'They won't hear it from me.'

'Thank you, sir.'

The headmaster wrote down his address and passed it to Herbert. 'Saturday morning, ten o'clock, sharp. Don't be late.'

Herbert put the paper in his pocket and left the room, walking past a jovial-looking Mr Stone.

'Good riddance, Finch,' said the science teacher with a smirk.

'Sorry, sir?'

'Knowing I won't be seeing your smug face around school next year has made my summer.'

He gave Herbert what was supposed to be a smile, although it was obviously something his face wasn't used to doing. In fact, it looked more like he was in desperate need of the toilet.

'I'm not going anywhere. You get to spend all of next year with me, sir. Won't that be fun? See you tomorrow,' Herbert sang, marching off to the sound of the headmaster's door slamming shut behind him.

He headed towards the exit, leaving Mr Stone to remonstrate with Mr Hucklebuck about the school prankster not being expelled.

Herbert walked outside and headed over to meet David, Brian and Trevor who were all waiting to hear the news.

'Cleaning his garage? For two days? That's all you got?' Trevor asked as they made their way home.

'No detention?' asked a shocked Brian.

Herbert shook his head.

David was next to quiz his friend. 'No cane. No expulsion?'

'Nope. Old Bony ain't happy.'

'Is he ever?' laughed Brian.

Trevor asked, 'So, lads, what's the plan for the summer?'

'Mischief,' replied Herbert, rubbing his hands together in excitement.

But he couldn't have been further from the truth. It was going to be a summer unlike any he'd ever experienced.

CHAPTER NINETEEN

Mr Hucklebuck's Garage

On Saturday morning at ten o'clock, Herbert stood in front of Mr Hucklebuck's garage. How was he expected to clear the contents of this in two days? It was chock-a-block. The headmaster had neglected to tell him it was in fact a double garage full to the brim with boxes and boxes of personal belongings. Herbert couldn't see how far back it went, but he knew it would take him a lot longer than two days.

He lifted the first box and it crumbled, spilling the contents onto the floor. Herbert raised his head skywards and sighed. He was now thinking that expulsion would have been the easier option.

He put the collapsed box to one side, picked up the spilled contents lying at his feet, and placed them on top. He grabbed the next box, taking care to support this one underneath, and placed it next to the first one. The boxes were flimsy and falling apart. Many were covered in mould and had signs of water damage. How was he supposed to repack any of this?

Herbert spent the next three hours sorting blankets, sheets, clothes and ornaments. There were pictures, kitchen utensils and broken toys. There was no end in sight.

He sat down for a break and took the contents out of the box nearest to him. That's when he saw it. In amongst the items was a magazine – a black racing car emblazoned across its front cover. The driver's goggles were covered in dirt and he had a grimace on his face.

Herbert flicked through, taking in photo after photo. He became lost in the articles and enjoyment displayed on the drivers' faces. He reached the last page and, instead of going back to work, took out another magazine. There were piles and piles of them, all about car racing, each cover full of excitement, enticing him to turn the page. He completely lost track of what he was meant to be doing.

'Busy?' came a voice from behind him, making Herbert jump to his feet and drop the magazine.

Mr Hucklebuck had emerged from his house and was standing just outside the garage door, a sandwich in one hand and a glass of juice in the other.

'I-I-I'm sorry, sir. I was just having a quick break.'

Herbert pushed the magazines back into the partially collapsed box and walked over to get another one from the pile.

'Herbert, relax. Take a seat,' smiled Mr Hucklebuck, motioning towards a bench.

'I'm sorry sir, I just …'

'Herbert, it's fine. There's no rush. This is your time, after all,' he said with a smile.

Herbert sat back down and Mr Hucklebuck passed him the sandwich and the juice.

The headmaster sat down next to Herbert. 'So, you like motor racing, do you?'

'I don't know, sir. I just saw the magazine and it looked interesting.'

'Oh, it is interesting! More than you can possibly imagine.'

'Do you like it, sir?'

'Indeed I do. I could have made it as a professional, if it wasn't for the accident …'

'*Accident*, sir?' asked a puzzled Herbert.

'I used to race, but then the war came and I had a nasty accident. I couldn't race again after that.'

'Why? What happened?'

The headmaster pulled up his left trouser leg to show several long scars. 'I got crushed. Torn ligaments, tendon damage, loss of feeling. I broke my tibia and fibula bones in the lower leg and needed six operations just to get it to work as well as it does. Not much good for being a racing driver.'

'So that's why you walk with a limp, sir?'

'*Limp?*' repeated Mr Hucklebuck, frowning. 'I don't limp.'

Herbert's cheeks flushed red. 'Oh, I'm sorry ...'

Mr Hucklebuck chuckled. 'Herbert, I'm joking. Yes, that's why I have a limp!'

Herbert was relieved. 'How did it happen?'

'A friend and I were moving rubble away after an air raid when a wall collapsed and fell right on top of us. My best friend was killed and I was trapped. At first it looked like I was going to lose my leg, but thankfully they managed to save it.'

The headmaster pulled his trouser leg back down and gave Herbert a tight-lipped smile, but his eyes displayed the pain of recalling the incident.

'That must've been awful,' sighed Herbert.

'It was. But, I'm still here. Many didn't make it out of the war. We should be thankful for small mercies.'

'Were you good, at racing, sir?'

'I was.'

'And you think you would have made it?'

'Without a doubt. I was going to be the best racing driver in the world,' said Mr Hucklebuck, with a bright smile.

'And there's no way you can drive now?'

Herbert took a bite of the sandwich. Cheese and pickle.

The headmaster replied, 'Oh, I can drive. But not to the standard needed to be the best, and nothing but the best was good enough for me. You need to have the edge, to take risks, to have quick reactions. Being in a racing car is no easy feat. You're locked inside a cockpit where the slightest mistake could cost you your life.'

'Were you not scared?'

'Every time I climbed in the car.'

'Then why do it?' Herbert asked, before sinking half the juice. Blackcurrant.

'For the buzz, of course! The excitement of pitting your wits against the best drivers around. Knowing each race could be your last. There was no better adrenaline rush.'

'Sounds scary. You wouldn't catch me doing that!'

'It was scary,' agreed Mr Hucklebuck, standing up. 'But you need to ask yourself one question, Herbert.'

'What's that, sir?'

The headmaster gave a knowing smile. 'If it's so dangerous and doesn't interest you, why have you been sitting here for the last twenty minutes engrossed in those magazines? Now, you'd best tidy this away before heading home. There's a pile of new boxes on the other side of the garage.'

Herbert walked over and pulled up the door that led to the second half of the garage. It made a rattling sound as it slid along the rollers attached to the roof. On the right-hand side there were flat-pack boxes, rolls of tape and a carton of marker pens. But Herbert wasn't looking at them. His eyes were firmly fixed on the item sitting in the middle of the space.

'It's a beauty isn't it?' came Mr Hucklebuck's voice.

'Is it yours?'

'Indeed it is.'

'Where did you get it?'

'My dad bought it for me,' said Mr Hucklebuck, shaking his head. 'After the accident I couldn't use it, but I couldn't get rid of it either. You like it?'

'It's amazing,' said Herbert, stepping forward and running his hand along the front of it.

'I thought you'd like it. You see, I know you, Herbert.'

'I should hope so, sir. I go to your school.'

Mr Hucklebuck smiled. 'You remind me of another child I once knew. You're so much like him, it's quite unnerving.'

Herbert turned. 'Surely there can't be another child as funny or as good-looking as me, sir?'

'You should have been expelled after the stunt you pulled this week. I should have called the police and had you charged with breaking and entering. You're a very lucky boy.'

'I know, sir. Thank you. Why didn't you expel me?'

'As I explained to you, it would be passing on the problem. And as much as you're a prankster, I think you have more to offer this world than you realise. Mind you, Mr Stone wasn't too impressed by my decision ...'

'What did he say after I left?'

'Told me I should have thrown you to the lions; be made an example of; said other students will think I'm soft and that they can get away with anything.'

'And what do you think, sir?' asked Herbert, taking a step towards the headmaster.

'I think what I'm about to suggest will show I was right about you all along.'

'Right about me, sir?'

'I'm going to conduct a little experiment.'

'Sounds ominous,' smiled Herbert.

'You have two choices. Your first is to finish tidying the garage, after which you can go and enjoy the summer with your friends and come back to school in September, when the punishment will be forgotten. You can then carry on along your previous path, messing about and squandering your education ...'

Herbert was intrigued. 'Or?'

'Or you can hang around here all summer and I can teach you everything I know. You can look around the garage and see what you can find.'

'What's the catch?'

'There's no catch. All you have to do is knuckle down, pass all your exams and stop skylarking, and you will have a bright future.'

'That sounds like a pretty big *catch* to me.'

'No, Herbert. It's what most children do in school, believe it or not!'

'Really? Weirdos.'

The headmaster smiled, shook his head and headed back towards the house.

Before he disappeared, Herbert shouted after him, 'Sir?'

Mr Hucklebuck turned around. 'Yes?'

'What happened to the other boy? You know, the one who used to be like me?'

'Oh, didn't I tell you?'

Herbert shook his head. 'No.'

'He grew up and became headmaster of the local school.'

Mr Hucklebuck winked, and then he was gone, leaving Herbert to contemplate what sort of future he wanted. One more look at the item in the headmaster's garage left him in little doubt.

Herbert was going to change his ways.

1962

CHAPTER TWENTY

Where Are We?

While Herbert was easing them to the ground, Jack peered out of the window, but the smoke from the jet engines was pluming upwards, engulfing the time machine and obscuring his view. He was still unsure what was going on with his grandad today. He'd been jittery since they'd taken off. In fact, he'd not been his normal, chatty, jokey self, at all. It was obvious the adventure he had planned for today was different to anything they'd experienced over the past four years together. It was also the first time their destination had been kept secret. The whole experience so far had been very strange indeed.

'Where are we, Grandad?'

'You'll find out soon enough, my boy,' answered Herbert, pressing buttons and twisting dials to bring the time machine safely to the ground.

The digital display was showing they were thirty metres from the ground. Red lights blinked away, illuminating the dashboard, while beeps and whirs signalled their descent. They would soon be on solid ground again.

Twenty metres.

The engines sounded like they were about to explode as they assisted the safe landing.

Fifteen metres.

The smoke continued to billow around them. It was the same landing routine every time, only this time Herbert was a lot more apprehensive.

Five metres.

The alarms beeped louder, the lights flashed brighter, and the roaring of the engines was more intense.

They rocked and bounced as they landed. The lights turned from red to green, the beeping ceased, and the engines switched from a deep rumble to a gentle purring, before dying completely.

Jack stood and walked over to the window. The smoke had cleared and all he could see were fields of green grass stretching far into the distance.

'Right, Jack,' said Herbert. 'You ready? Don't forget the sweets.'

Herbert straightened himself, pushed the door open and stepped outside.

There wasn't a building or a road in sight. As Jack closed his eyes and filled his nostrils with the sweet aroma of freshly cut grass, a faint buzzing sound filled his ears. At first, he thought he was still recovering from the noise of the jets, but then he realised it was coming from somewhere in the distance.

'Where are we?' asked Jack.

'We're back in the best year of my life.'

'1962?'

'Indeed.'

'Why?'

'Because there's something I want to show you. Something I hope you'll enjoy.'

'What is it?'

Herbert smiled and shook his head. 'All in good time.'

He turned on his heels and headed to the other side of the time machine. Jack followed him around the corner and came to an abrupt halt. Right there, at the end of the field in which they'd landed in, was a concrete building.

Jack asked, 'What's that?'

Herbert didn't answer; he was already marching forwards, beckoning over his shoulder for Jack to follow. There was the faint smell of burning rubber and, in the distance, more smoke billowed from the other side of the building. There was that sound again, and Jack recognised what it was: screeching tyres. This time, it was accompanied by the roaring of a crowd.

Where had grandad brought them? And more importantly, why were they here?

Herbert was on a mission, striding onwards like he was late for a very important meeting. Jack had to do a funny half-run, half-walk shuffle to keep up.

As they got closer Jack heard another sound: an announcer. His voice was faint, but Jack made out two words: 'big race'.

'Grandad, will you slow down and tell me what's going on?'

Herbert didn't slow down, he didn't check his stride, and he didn't answer. He was in a world of his own, arms swinging with each step. Jack shook his head and forgot about trying to discover why they were here. No doubt he would find out soon enough.

Jack was breathless. He wasn't sure if it was because of the excitement, or the speed walk his grandad had taken them on. They were now only twenty metres from the concrete building, and the crowd were getting louder, cheering and chanting away.

Herbert stopped marching and turned.

'Right, Jack. Here we are,' he said, pointing towards the building looming above them. 'Like I said, this was a very important year for me – a very important day, in fact – so I wanted you to see it.'

Jack nodded.

Herbert removed a handkerchief from his trouser pocket and wiped his brow. 'This place here,' he said, motioning towards the building, 'is where I spent many happy hours. It was my sanctuary. The time I spent in Mr Hucklebuck's garage unlocked something inside of me. A passion, a fire – a determination I can't describe. I spent weeks at his house. Time spent with my friends became less and less frequent.'

Jack removed a bottle of water from his bag, unscrewed the lid and passed it to his gasping grandad, who gulped down the contents.

'Thank you.'

'I thought you only had to work there for two days?' asked Jack, replacing the lid and returning the bottle to his bag.

Herbert nodded and wiped his mouth with the back of his hand. 'I did, but something happened during those two days that made me want to stay. I told Mr Hucklebuck that I hadn't quite finished. I had, of course, and he knew I had, but I wanted to stay a bit longer because of what I'd discovered. Mr Hucklebuck smiled when I asked him. He knew I'd dragged the job out. Not because I was lazy, but because I was enjoying my time there.'

'What did he say?'

'He said I could go there as much as I wanted, as long as I cleared it with my parents. He also made one other thing very clear.'

'What was that?' asked Jack, now transfixed.

'If my schoolwork suffered, if my grades weren't up to scratch, or if I got into any more trouble, I would never be allowed in his garage again.'

'What did you do?'

Herbert stood tall. 'I became the best-behaved boy in school. My homework was always handed in on time, and my attitude towards my education improved overnight. My whole outlook changed, all because of those few weeks spent in Mr Hucklebuck's garage.'

'But why?' asked Jack. 'What was in Mr Hucklebuck's garage that was so fantastic it made you change?'

He was hoping to finally discover the secret that made his grandad want to take them back fifty years, and to this specific place.

Herbert smiled. 'I'll show you.'

CHAPTER TWENTY-ONE

Jack's Surprise

They reached the main concourse at the front of the building where noise was rumbling through the crowd; everyone talking excitedly about what could happen today. The hairs on the back of Jack's neck stood on end; something special was clearly going on, but he didn't know what. One thing he did know, was that they were most definitely at a racetrack.

The smell of acrid smoke, combined with the throaty growl of car engines, filled the air. Jack looked to his left where there was a grandstand filled to the brim with bustling, excited spectators. Red flags stood proud at either end of the roof and gently swayed in the breeze. TV filming towers were dotted all around: the old-fashioned cameras positioned at the top were being swept from side to side by the cameramen operating them.

'Right, it might be a little noisy when we go in here,' Herbert warned, hitching his thumb towards the building. 'So, if it's too much, let me know and we'll leave. Okay?'

It was already noisy, but there was no way Jack was going to say he wanted to leave, even if it was too loud inside. This was obviously important to his grandad, so that made it important to Jack, too.

'Deal,' said Jack.

'Good boy. Right. Follow me!'

They walked through the main doors, and there was an explosion of noise. Drivers were dotted everywhere, all wearing white overalls that displayed the badges of their sponsors. Some were huddled in groups – presumably discussing the upcoming 'big race' – while others had a more relaxed attitude: a drink in one hand and a beautiful girl pulled in tight with the other. Some were speaking to reporters, and more on the far side were having their photographs taken or signing memorabilia for their fans.

Herbert reached down and grabbed Jack's right hand. This was something he'd not done on any of their previous adventures.

Jack frowned at him.

'Whatever happens, I don't want you to panic,' Herbert said and smiled. 'Everything is going to be just fine.'

Jack followed his grandad through the crowds – literally, right through people, like they always did when time-travelling.

They moved towards the far end of the building, where the racetrack was situated behind a wall of glass. The sun came bursting through, temporarily blinding Jack. He closed his eyes and brought his free hand up to protect them.

Moments later, when the sun moved behind a cloud, Jack lowered his hand – and was instantly overcome with excitement. Cars were zooming around the track at great speeds, producing ear-piercing *vrooms* as they sped past. Jack took in the different sounds; the roar of the crowd, the screeching of tyres. There was an almighty crash as a car flew off the track and smashed into the safety barriers.

Herbert asked, 'What do you think?'

'This is amazing!' beamed Jack. 'No wonder you wanted to come here today, Grandad!'

'You wanna get a closer look?'

'Yeah!'

'We could sneak down there,' suggested Herbert, pointing to their left.

'What's that?'

'That's the pit lane. It's where all the teams prepare their cars and drivers before they head out onto the track to race; change tyres, refuel cars, carry out repairs. It all happens down there!'

'Really?'

'You wanna go?'

'Definitely – but I thought we could anyway. We can go anywhere, right?'

Herbert gave a wry smile. 'Indeed we can.'

The crowd in the main stands roared, encouraging their favourite drivers, and berating their nearest rivals. Jack couldn't see clearly because of the amount of people wandering around the concourse.

'Don't let go of my hand,' instructed Herbert.

Jack nodded. He knew they were not in any danger. They were invisible and he knew his way back to the time machine if they became separated – although the thought of getting lost still made him feel anxious.

He followed close behind his grandad, keeping a tight hold of his hand as they walked through the crowd to reach the pit lane situated right next to the track. Cars were flying past in colours of racing green, fire red, deep blue, jet black and sunflower yellow; their tyres screeching when they slowed for the corners, before banking around at speed and exiting right on the edge of the track. Some misjudged the bend and went flying into the barriers. Car after car zoomed along, making the same ear-splitting *shriek*. The drivers were pushing the cars to their limits.

Herbert looked down and mouthed, 'Are you okay?'

Jack nodded.

People walked past them as well as right through them. They'd never been anywhere so crowded. An announcement poured from the speakers dotted around the track. This time, Jack heard every word.

'Next up, ladies and gentlemen, it's the one you've all been waiting for. The race you're all here to see. The big climax! It's time for the final race of the season and the stakes couldn't be any higher!'

The crowd erupted and began shouting and cheering.

Herbert's hand, which was now becoming sweaty due to the heat, gripped Jack's even tighter and pulled him onwards. Row upon row of people lined the track.

'Okay,' added the announcer, 'ladies and gents, refill your drinks, take that toilet break, and get back to your seats or find a place to watch this next one. The drivers will soon be making their way to the pit lane. What an amazing spectacle this is going to be! Let's hope it ends in a British victory!'

Jack stopped and watched the crowd as they cheered even louder.

'Raiser! Raiser! Raiser! Raiser!'

Jack had no idea who the crowd were chanting for, but the hairs on the back of his neck were, once again, standing on end. This was exhilarating. He now understood why his grandad was so excited about coming back to this moment in time. The atmosphere was electric.

Herbert tugged Jack's arm, and they were moving again. In the rush, Jack's hand slipped from his grandad's, but only for a split second before Herbert grabbed it again. Suddenly, Jack's body began to tingle and something very unusual happened, making his heart jump – somebody bumped into him.

'Sorry, fella,' the man said. Then another nudged him, followed by another, and another. It was like he was actually in among the crowd for real but, if he and his grandad were invisible, how could this be happening?

Jack gripped his grandad's hand tighter. At least, he thought it was his grandad's hand, but it wasn't soft and gentle. This was a strong, smooth, determined hand pulling Jack along. He looked up. The man guiding him didn't look at all like his slightly hunched over, grey-haired grandad. This tall man had jet-black hair and, even from behind, Jack could sense he had presence.

Jack wasn't holding Herbert's hand, and he was no longer invisible. He was here for real. In the flesh. He spun around but couldn't see his grandad anywhere and he began to panic. He'd only let go for a split second and now he was being pulled away, becoming lost in the bustling crowd with no idea of where his grandad had gone.

Jack tried to free his own hand from the stranger's, but the grip was too tight. He wanted to call out for someone to help him but, in his panicked state, he couldn't get his words out; they were stuck in his throat. He continued to bounce off people, apologies fired at him from every angle.

'Sorry, little man.'

'You shouldn't be in here, it's too dangerous.'

'Careful, fella.'

'I almost stepped on you there!'

Jack couldn't respond to any of them: in the blink of an eye, they walked past him and were gone. He wanted to reach out and tell them he'd been snatched by this stranger, but his arm wouldn't move the way he wanted it to.

They were nearing the entrance to the pit lane. Maybe he would see his grandad inside? Jack looked from left to right, searching for a member of staff, a police officer, anyone who could help him escape from this man. But there was nobody he could ask!

They reached the pit lane entrance and the security guard let them through, smiling at the stranger and nodding to Jack. He needed to escape. He yanked his arm as hard as he could, hoping the element of surprise would work. It did. Jack's hand slipped free and he turned to run but was immediately grabbed by the collar and pulled through the open doorway of a small, empty room. He went to cry out, but a hand covered his mouth, gripping it firmly enough to keep the scream at bay.

'I know this is a shock, but calm down, Jack, my boy,' said the stranger.

Jack froze. Only one person in the world called him 'Jack, my boy,' and that was his grandad. Jack stopped fighting and the hand around his mouth relaxed.

He turned his head and studied the stranger. At a guess, he was in his mid-twenties. Wild, dark hair rested on two broad shoulders. His arms and chest looked strong enough to carry a tree trunk, and his legs looked like they were carved from stone.

Jack looked into the man's deep-blue eyes and, even without the dark droopy bags underneath them, he recognised them instantly. 'Grandad?'

Herbert winked and smiled. 'I think you deserve an explanation.'

CHAPTER TWENTY-TWO

The Trailer

The buzz of the crowd, the roar of the engines and the screeching of tyres filled the air, but all Jack could concentrate on was the sight of his grandad as a young man. He couldn't believe what was happening; they'd never done anything like this before. They'd explored the most amazing places in the world, safe in the knowledge they were never in any danger, thanks to how they'd travelled. But now that had all changed. They were at the racetrack, like two regular spectators.

After recovering from the initial shock, Jack followed Herbert to a trailer behind the main stand. He climbed the three metal steps and entered, while his grandad disappeared to grab some food.

There was a metal sink in the corner with two towels hanging over the side. A brown leather bag, unzipped, with clothes poking out, lay on a small sofa next to it. The beige walls were full of pictures and newspaper articles of racing cars, drivers, and tracks from around the world. There was something familiar about the cars, but Jack couldn't think what, exactly.

The door opened and Herbert walked in, armed with drinks and sandwiches.

'Hungry?'

'Starving.'

'Okay, sit yourself down and I'll explain what's going on. We don't have long, so I best be quick.'

Jack lifted the top off his sandwich to inspect it; he didn't like surprises in his food.

Herbert noticed and chuckled. 'Don't worry, it's only cheese and ham.'

Jack replaced the top and took a bite. His eyes continued taking in the memorabilia on the walls before finally settling on a newspaper cutting. He couldn't read the report, but the headline was in bold black letters: 'Raiser does it again!'

'So,' began Herbert, drawing Jack's attention away from the article. 'I guess there are a few questions rolling around in that head of yours?'

Jack had a mouthful of food, so simply nodded.

'Okay,' said Herbert, placing his sandwich down and motioning around the trailer. 'This was my life when I was younger. During the summer I spent clearing out Mr Hucklebuck's garage, I discovered all sorts of driving memorabilia: posters, model cars, old racing overalls and various other racing-related items. I read every single article I found. I'm not sure what it was about it, but I was hooked, right from the start. The first time Mr Hucklebuck came out to check on me and found me sitting down reading a racing magazine, I thought I was in big trouble, but he smiled and came to talk to me. He wasn't in headmaster mode, not in his own house. He was more like a friendly uncle. I ended up going there every evening throughout the summer holidays and we'd sit and talk about racing.'

Herbert paused and took a sip of water, giving Jack the opportunity to take it all in.

Jack asked, 'What has this got to do with what's happening here?'

'I'm getting to that bit ...'

Jack took another bite of his sandwich. It tasted so good. He wasn't sure if it was because he was hungry or excited by the story.

'Well, like I said, I read all the newspaper articles and magazines I found in the garage. I read them over and over again, absorbing every single word. I knew right then what I wanted to be when I was old enough. Mr Hucklebuck would sit and tell me all about the thrill of watching drivers throwing their cars around bends at high speed. I could tell how disappointed he was at not being able to drive himself, but it never stopped him from encouraging me.'

'What happened?'

'I knuckled down in school, improved my grades and became the best version of me I could be. Monday to Friday it was studying and putting my schoolwork first. No more skylarking or messing around; I would have plenty of time for that when I was older. From the moment I walked into Mr Hucklebuck's garage, my life and attitude changed.'

The announcer's voice came again, and Jack could make out two words – 'Twenty minutes' – followed by another roar from the crowd.

Herbert stood and opened the door. The noise level increased as he poked his head out and took a quick look around. 'Right, Jack, we need to get going.'

'What? Where? Are we going home already?'

Herbert smiled, 'Oh, no. We haven't even started yet.'

Jack couldn't understand what was going on. 'Grandad, I get that you wanted to come back here, but you haven't explained how we're actually here – *physically*, I mean. Why are we not invisible like we normally are?'

'Okay,' Herbert sighed and sat back down. 'A few years ago, just before you were born, I was digging around in the loft, trying to find an old photograph album that your grandma wanted, when I stumbled across some of my old scrap books. I sat there for a couple of hours flicking through them, and it brought the memories flooding back. I began reminiscing about this time in my life and what an important part it had played. That's what made me want to come back here. I hadn't even thought about it until then. It was a lifetime ago, after all. So anyway, I was all set to return, but then you came along and everything changed. I decided to wait until you were old enough so I could bring you with me. Although, I couldn't risk anything bad happening to you. As you can see, this is no place for a little boy. I would never have forgiven myself if it all went wrong.'

'You could have come on your own.'

Herbert recoiled and sat up straight as if he'd been scolded. 'Without you? Fat chance.'

Jack smiled. 'So, are you a transformer or something? I mean, you look so much younger?

Herbert chuckled. 'Not quite.' He reached down and pulled up his sleeve. 'It's all down to this.'

'Whoa!' Jack gasped. 'What's that?'

On Herbert's wrist was the coolest thing Jack had ever seen. Behind the glass face of an oval-shaped watch were two round dials. The watch's electric-blue background was illuminated by crackling bolts of lightning which served as the hands within each dial. The first dial contained a single lightning bolt which was spinning so quickly it was difficult to see it. The second dial had six crackling hands moving slowly in an anti-clockwise direction, chasing each other around the clock-face. But it was what was underneath these dials that drew Jack's attention. Sitting there, crackling away, were two lines of lightning-style text.

Jack read aloud. '1962. Physical self. What does that mean?'

'This is a time-traveller's watch,' Herbert explained. 'This is how we can change form.'

'*Form?*' queried Jack.

'Yes. How we can change from being invisible, *or non-corporeal*, as it is known, to being our own physical selves, or *corporeal* as it's called. Like we are now ...'

'How does it work?' asked Jack.

'Well, this one here,' Herbert said, tapping the dial containing the single lightning bolt, 'let's us know the portal is still open and ready for our return ... and this one,' he motioned at the second clockface, 'is maintaining the functions of the time machine.'

'What about this?' asked Jack, pointing at the text.

'Ah, now this one shows our current form. Like when we become invisible,' added Herbert, his eyes wide with excitement.

Jack smirked, 'Don't you mean *non-corporeal*, Grandad?'

Herbert smiled and ruffled Jack's hair. 'That's right. You're a fast learner, my boy!'

'But how does it actually work?'

Herbert turned his wrist and pointed to the side of the watch. 'You see this button here?'

Jack looked closer. There was a small black rubber button. 'Yes.'

'This is the control switch.'

'*Control switch?*'

Herbert nodded. 'Give it a twist clockwise.'

Jack grabbed the button between his thumb and index finger and turned it in a clockwise direction. There was a click and the two lines – '1962. Physical self.' – fizzed and crackled before a bolt of lightning flashed across the display, changing the text to read: '2012. Invisible.' Jack gasped as his grandad instantly disappeared then reappeared moments later with the biggest grin on his face.

Herbert offered the watch back to Jack. Without hesitation he turned the switch clockwise, twice. There were two clicks this time. The text changed again: '2012. Physical self.' Jack watched Herbert flicker and crackle before transforming back into the 74-year-old grandad he visited every week.

'Wh–wh–what the–' Jack stammered.

Herbert turned the switch again and, as the text changed back to '1962. Physical self.', he became his younger self once more.

'Pretty cool, huh?'

'How does it do that?' gasped Jack.

'I programmed it before you arrived this morning,' replied Herbert, sounding like it was the most impressive thing he'd ever managed.

'Where did you get it?' asked Jack, his wide-eyed gaze fixed on the special watch that had turned his grandad's biological clock back fifty years.

'When the time machine was left to me, this was inside with a set of instructions. It's quite easy really, and essential for things like this, don't you think?'

Jack took a sharp intake of breath as the realisation hit him. 'That was why you let go of my hand! You quickly changed into your younger self and then grabbed my hand again!'

Herbert nodded. 'I was so nervous. I didn't know what you'd think. I'm so sorry I scared you, but I wanted it all to be a big surprise. Maybe it wasn't the best decision.'

Jack smiled. 'It's okay, I forgive you, Grandad. There is one thing though ...'

'What's that?'

'How did I become my physical self again? Y'know, when we were walking through the crowd?'

Herbert shrugged. 'I guess I must have transferred some of the watch's energy to you when I grabbed your hand. I had no idea it was going to do that,' Herbert huffed. 'Good job you didn't turn into a ball of smoke!'

'So, you don't use it all the time?'

'No. I only ever use it if I want to change form; something I've done many times when I travel on my own.'

'That's so awesome!' said Jack.

'Anyway,' Herbert added, 'I have to disappear in a minute but my friend, Patrick, will be here to look after you.'

'Where are you going?'

'I have something important to do.'

Herbert reached into his pocket and removed an envelope. He turned it over in his hands and then held it out to Jack. 'I hope this will help to explain things.'

Jack took the envelope and watched the younger version of his grandad stand and stretch. He couldn't believe what a giant of a man he'd been in his youth. It was funny to think that this strong man was actually a seventy-four-year old grandad who loved nothing more than winding up his wife.

Herbert paused with his hand on the door handle. 'Patrick will be here before long. In the meantime,' said Herbert nodding at the envelope, 'read that and I'll see you soon.'

And with that, he was gone. The door closed and Jack was left with nothing but an old, tatty envelope and the buzz of excitement from outside. Although, he couldn't hear any of it. Not really. All he could hear were his own thoughts racing around inside his head. What on earth was going on? Maybe the contents of the envelope would hold the answer?

Jack turned the envelope over and saw one faded word scrawled on the front: '*Herbie*'. Jack opened it and pulled out a flimsy sheet of paper that looked like it might fall apart at any moment. He gently unfolded it and read it while he waited for Patrick to arrive. And when he did, Jack would find out all about his grandad's secret, and it would be far bigger than he could have ever thought possible.

Jack was in for the shock of his life.

CHAPTER TWENTY-THREE

William's Letter

Dearest Herbert,

First of all, I feel I must apologise for not telling you the truth about this whole situation. But, in my defence, if I'd said you were having a conversation with a dead person, well, you might have phoned the psychiatric hospital to see if they'd lost a patient – I know I would have! I can only imagine what you must be thinking, so I'll do my best to alleviate any fears and concerns you may have. There's a lot to explain, so I'll keep it short.

I appreciate you agreeing to take custody of the time machine. Obviously, it's for slightly longer than a month. Sorry about that. It took me a long time to find somebody, I felt, was suited to the task ahead, but I'm confident I've made the right choice.

You see, this time machine has been around for years, centuries in fact, and when the current custodian nears the end of their life, they need to transfer ownership to whomever they deem suitable. Each custodian must have a certain set of values, including, but not limited to: integrity, honesty, loyalty, morality and, above all else, trustworthiness. After watching you closely over the years, I'm confident you contain all of these positive traits, if not more.

Now, the problem with having to hand over custody of the time machine is that you must be alive to complete the process and, as I was tragically killed before this was possible, it left me in a bit of a quandary. I needed to transfer ownership before I could be released from this life. Those are the rules. So, for the best part of a year, I was, to put it in layman's terms, floating around the ether, like a ghost. The only person I was to converse with was whoever I'd chosen to take ownership! That meant I needed to be sure I'd made the right choice. And after the fun I'd had over the years, I wasn't going to leave her to just anybody.

I took my time, and travelled to all corners of the earth, looking for a suitable candidate. Some seemed to be perfect, but then something would happen which would bring their suitability into question, and I had to reject them. I began losing faith until I found you. Herbert Finch: the man that everybody loved. So, I followed you and observed you over a period of time, with a few trips back to your past, of course. I watched the way you treated your friends, the respect and love you showed your wife and the unconditional love you had for your daughter, helping her to grow and mature. Nothing was too much trouble for you and, although you like to play the goat, act the funny man and try to wind people up, it is quite clear that you're … how can I put it? Ah, yes, a big softie with a heart of gold.

You were the one I chose. I knew she would be in safe hands. So, I arranged for Jasmine's school to visit the museum. I also made sure that you were certain to get a space on the trip as a supervisor. Don't ask me how. It's a secret! Once you were there, the rest was easy.

There was one thing I didn't tell you during our little adventure: the time-traveller's watch. It is imperative that you get to grips with its functions. I've no doubt there will be certain trips where you will wish to change your appearance, or even aspects of the trip. This was the whole reason I was able to bring back the doorway to the basement. It also allowed me to return and transfer ownership of the time machine. You'll find the watch, along with some instructions, inside the drawer under the dashboard. Please be careful with it, Herbie!

So, now it's over to you. You're the custodian. You're the one who is to determine how and when she can be used and, ultimately, you will be responsible for handing her over when the time comes.

So, there you have it. Take care of her, keep her safe and don't forget your maintenance checks. We don't want you falling out of the sky, again!

Thank you, and I hope you have as much fun as I did over the years.

Until we meet again, my friend.

Best wishes,

William

CHAPTER TWENTY-FOUR

Where's Herbie?

Herbert left his trailer, turned the corner, and was immediately dazzled by an explosion of lightbulbs. He squinted and raised his hand, pushing his way through the crowds. It may well have been fifty years since he'd experienced the clamour surrounding him, but he remembered it like it was only yesterday. The cameras, the fans chanting his name and the reporters desperate for a headline, made the hairs on the back of his neck stand on end.

There were so many times he wanted to come back here, but he couldn't, not without Jack. This was one of the most important days of Herbert's life and he couldn't think of anyone else he would rather spend it with. After all, this would be one of their last trips together. Herbert wasn't getting any younger, and the journeys into the past were really starting to take their toll.

The lightbulbs continued to flash, and a microphone was shoved in his face.

'So, Herbie, how are you feeling? You must be so excited about today?' asked one reporter.

'Today's the culmination of years of work; how do you think you'll feel when it's all over?' asked another.

The next one was straight to the point. 'Can you do it, Herbie?'

Herbert pushed his way through, head down, deep in thought, and entered the sanctuary of the pit lane.

The track was on the right with the cars lined up along the left. Mechanics were carrying out their final checks and making any necessary last-minute adjustments. It all looked so different, yet so familiar. Herbert had wound the clock back fifty years; his heart was racing and his palms were sweating.

He reached the garage and saw the nose of it poking out. The white circle sitting at the front with the black '10' in the centre of it made his heart skip a beat. The mechanics were being meticulous in checking the car and making sure it was ready, right down to the finest detail. This was a big day and they couldn't afford to take any chances. Of course, Herbert knew it would be perfect and drive just as it should. One mechanic was leaning into the cockpit and pressing the accelerator pedal. The engine roared into life before dropping to a gentle purring sound.

The final checks were complete and the car was moved onto the track. This was it. This was the moment. Herbert couldn't tell Jack what he'd planned for today; it would have ruined the surprise.

Herbert walked to the back of the garage and slipped into his overalls. He took a deep breath, picked up his helmet and followed his mechanics onto the track.

It was time.

There was a knock on the trailer door.

'Jack?' came a voice as the door opened. 'I'm Patrick, I'm here to take you to see Herbie.'

'Where is he?' inquired Jack, placing William's letter in his bag.

'He's busy at the moment, but I'm going to look after you until he's free.'

Jack nodded and stood.

Patrick asked, 'So, I understand you're a friend of the family? We don't normally let children get so close, but he was adamant you should be allowed in. I like your clothes. Is this the latest fashion?'

He looked Jack up and down and smiled awkwardly.

Jack realised his jeans, Nike trainers and red hoody would appear strange to someone from fifty years ago. 'Umm, yeah, it's all new. A sort of prototype ... new lines, y'know?'

Patrick nodded, but looked unconvinced.

'Anyway, what's going on?' Jack asked. 'Where's ... umm ... Herbie?' It felt weird calling his grandad by his nickname, but he couldn't very well call him Grandad: he was only twenty-four.

'He's tied up at the moment, but we'll see him soon. My instructions were to collect you and look after you,' replied Patrick. 'So, if you're ready, let's go.'

Jack followed Patrick out of the trailer, squinting as the sunlight hit his eyes. The sound of engines revving, and the smell of oil came drifting over. They made their way through the throng of reporters and spectators rushing around, talking excitedly about today being a big day in British sport.

Patrick asked, 'So, Jack, do you like motor sport?'

'Yeah. I've never been to a live race before, though.' He was about to add how much he loved watching it on TV and would often sit with his dad who consumed every race on Sky Sports. But, considering Sky wasn't even invented yet, he thought it might not go down too well.

They passed under a canopy and into the paddock area where all the teams were gathered. The cars were right there on the track in front of them. The engines roared, and the mechanics were running here and there, tools in their hands and sweat pouring from their faces.

'So, what do you do, Patrick?' asked Jack.

'Oh, anything really. I have to sort out the after-race functions, look after guests, ensure the drivers get whatever they need ... That sort of stuff.'

'Does Herbie work in the garage?'

'Yes, he works with the mechanics.'

Jack was so excited. His grandad worked for a racing team! He wondered whether he could meet any of the drivers afterwards or sit in one of the cars. That would be so cool.

'Right, almost there. Stay close,' advised Patrick.

They pushed between a couple of mechanics who were shouting at each other – something about one of them being 'a baboon'. Their voices continued to rise as Jack eased through.

He glanced to his right. The cars were all ready. Drivers were climbing in, putting on their helmets and getting final instructions. The announcer's voice let everyone know that the race would be commencing in five minutes.

Everything looked so different from 2012. The drivers didn't wear an all-in-one helmet, only a strap fastened under the chin, leaving the face exposed. They also wore goggles – no visors covering the whole face. Their overalls were looser and didn't offer the same protection from fire as those used nowadays. There were no sponsorship stickers emblazoned all over the cars, the drivers' seating positions were more elevated and everything was more open. Jack couldn't help but think the cars of today looked so much safer – and faster.

'Here we are,' said Patrick, coming to a stop beside a crowd of people.

'Where's Gr— Herbie. *Where's Herbie?*' Jack corrected himself.

'Oh, you'll see him in a minute.'

Jack turned towards the track. Mechanics were swarming all over the twenty gleaming cars lined up on the starting grid. A bright yellow car was sitting at the front, with a dark green one beside it. Two identical black cars, that reminded Jack of giant beetles, were on the next row, followed by a gold car and another green. All the cars were purring expectantly.

Jack asked, 'Which team are we?'

'That one over there,' Patrick replied, pointing towards the middle of the pack.

Four mechanics were working on a bright red car with a big '10' on the front of it. Two were checking the tyres, another was working on the back of the car and the final member had one hand on the driver's helmet while he cleaned his goggles with a cloth.

A smile broke out over Jack's face. This was going to be amazing! He hoped his grandad could watch the race with him. Unless he was a member of the pit crew? That would be incredible. Imagine being so close to the racing drivers!

There was a sudden flurry and the mechanics ran from the track. The drivers pumped their pedals and a wave of roaring engines exploded. The crowd erupted in anticipation and excitement.

Jack's eyes continued to dart around, looking for any sign of his grandad, but he was nowhere to be seen. Team members in the garage behind him were running around gesticulating with their hands while mechanics and race directors talked race strategy. At the rear of the garage stood a group of four people who were definitely not part of the pit crew. Two men and two women, dressed in the colourful floral outfits Jack had seen many people wearing outside, were talking among themselves, while making sure they didn't impede the team members rushing about.

Patrick gently placed a hand on Jack's shoulder. 'How're you doing, young man?'

Jack beamed. 'Fantastic. This is so exciting!'

Patrick smiled and patted Jack on the shoulder.

The cars were set, the track was clear and the race was just moments from starting.

'Where's Herbie? Is he actually a mechanic?' Jack asked, eyes alive with excitement at the thought of his grandad being an integral part of the team.

Patrick looked over at the cars and back to Jack. 'Not quite a *mechanic.*'

'What do you mean? I thought he was part of the team?'

'He is part of the team, and he does work with the mechanics, as well as the pit crew.'

On the track, the cars revved even louder – they were getting ready. Smoke poured from their chrome exhaust pipes and the cars rocked from side to side.

'Look, they're about to start the race. You remember which one we are?'

'Number 10,' said Jack, pointing towards it.

'Yep! That's who we're cheering for, along with the rest of the crowd. He's our number one driver,' added Patrick. 'We also have number 15, but he's right at the back.'

More revving, more smoke. The atmosphere from the crowd reached a crescendo. They were eagerly waiting for the race to start. Jack watched on, unblinking, gripping the railings that separated spectators from the track. The blue sky above the start line was partially hidden behind plumes of acrid smoke, which poured from the gleaming exhaust pipes before dissipating in the air. The flag from the race starter rose into the air. It paused for what felt like forever, and then, in a series of swift movements, it was being waved enthusiastically and they were off!

An explosion of different colours burst from the starting grid. Smoke filled the air, tyres squealed and the cars wobbled as the drivers fought with the tarmac for traction. Immediately, the red number 10 weaved its way past two cars.

'Yes!' yelled Jack, punching the air. A dark green car lost control, spun and collided with a bright yellow car. Both vehicles danced across the track to the barriers, where they came to an abrupt halt. Smoke billowed from the wreckage. Race marshals, armed with fire extinguishers, jumped the barriers and doused the engines before they exploded.

The remaining cars reached the first corner; more screeching pierced the air and smoke poured from the track as they applied their brakes. The smell of burning rubber drifted up from the cars weaving in and out and trying to get past those in front, as well as avoiding cars behind who were trying the same tactics. Jack didn't realise it, but he was holding his breath.

The noise of the crowd drowned out the engines as the cars rounded the first corner and disappeared into the distance. Jack was gripped, the cars may have gone, but they would come back round, again and again, for the next couple of hours.

'How was that, Jack?'

Jack had forgotten Patrick was there. He looked up, beaming. 'Amazing. I never thought it would be so good!'

'They'll be back around in a minute. Keep looking over there and you'll see them. The crowd will let you know when they're approaching.'

'How long does it take to complete a lap?'

'Just under two minutes, give or take.'

Jack nodded and turned to face the corner. He brought his hand up to shade his eyes from the blazing sun.

The cars could still be heard in the distance, although they were much quieter now. Jack waited; it seemed to be taking forever. But then he heard the crowd. The roar was on the far side, but it was moving towards him like a Mexican wave. It rippled, getting louder and louder, just like the cars. The roar of engines was building as they approached. Jack spotted the lead car, it flashed around a corner up ahead. He craned his neck to see who it was, but lost sight of him when the chasing pack entered his view, hunting the leader.

The cars weaved their way through a series of twisting corners on their way towards the long straight to complete the first lap. A blur of the most beautiful colours poured around the final bend and, then, they were on the home straight.

Jack watched the lead car – the bright yellow one with a big black '4' inside a large white circle – work its way towards the line and complete the first lap. Behind it, by the smallest of margins, was the green car, number 6. Next was a jet-black car with a black '20' in a white circle. Car after car entered the straight as they manoeuvred their way around the twisting track, and then the crowd in the main stand erupted: this was their champion!

A flash of red was flying towards them, right behind a dark blue car. They rounded the final corner and, as they exited, the red car – number 10 – glided effortlessly past the blue one, number 14.

'Yes!' hollered Jack, punching the air again.

And then it started.

The crowd were on their feet, chanting 'Herbie! Herbie! Herbie! Herbie!'

Jack frowned, and then it hit him. He turned to Patrick and threw him a quizzical look. Patrick didn't say a word, he simply nodded. Jack gasped. His grandad was a part of the team, but he wasn't a mechanic, or a member of the pit crew. He was

223

their number one driver! Jack was bursting with pride. He turned back to the track, grinned, and joined the crowd.

'Herbie! Herbie! Herbie!' he screamed from the top of his lungs, bouncing up and down with excitement and cheering his grandad, the famous racing driver.

CHAPTER TWENTY-FIVE

The Race

Jack couldn't take his eyes off the track as the race continued at an exhilarating pace. There were so many questions he wanted to ask Patrick, but he didn't want to miss a single second of the action; he wanted to cheer his grandad all the way, whether he could see him or not.

After an hour of breath-taking racing, which saw the drivers constantly jostling for positions, only twenty laps remained. The crowd had been electric from the first moment, especially whenever the red number 10 came flying around the corner.

The four people in floral clothing, who had been standing at the back of the garage, had made their way to the front to watch the race unfold. They were going bananas, particularly when Herbert rounded the corner and zoomed past them, down the home straight. Whenever he appeared, one of the ladies screamed from the top of her lungs, clapping enthusiastically, and telling him he could do it. Jack smiled. Is that what he looked like: a crazed fan?

After starting the race in twelfth place, Herbert had moved up to eighth. He was still a way down the field, but he was keeping pace with the leaders. They'd pushed their cars as hard as they could – driving on the edge and risking crashing out of the race whenever there was the slightest opportunity of overtaking; no matter how dangerous it may be. Lap after lap after lap ticked by as the race reached its climax.

By the time there were only nine laps remaining, Herbert had climbed another place, to seventh.

'Okay, Jack, not long now! We need Herbie to win today to clinch the championship. Anything less may not be good enough,' said Patrick.

'What do you mean?'

'Well, points are awarded to the top six drivers in each race during the season. The driver with the most points at the end of the season wins the championship. If Herbie wins today he'll be crowned world champion!'

'So he has to come first today to win the championship?' asked Jack.

Patrick shook his head. 'Not necessarily; he could still win it by coming second or third, but it would depend on where his closest rivals finished. Only two cars can beat his points total, and they would need to finish either first or second today.'

Jack asked, 'Who are his rivals?'

'The green number 6 and the black number 20,' Patrick answered. 'They're both ahead of him at the moment, but there's a long way to go yet ...'

The roar of the crowd increased as the cars returned. Where was Herbert now? The first car was attacking the winding set of corners leading into the home straight. Jack noticed the big black '6' on the front of the green car. The lead had changed. A flash of black, number 20, followed, with the yellow car, number 4, now down in third. Jack was standing on his tiptoes, trying to get a better view. Another green car came into view. Four cars down with no sign of Herbert and laps were running out. Behind them there was a flash of gold with a big '8' on its bonnet, and then, there it was, the bright red car: number 10. Jack squealed, along with the crowd; Herbert was up to sixth, he'd picked off another car and was right on the tail of the gold number 8! By now, Jack was jumping up and down. The crowd screamed louder. They could sense something special was about to happen!

Herbert followed the gold car around the last corner, right on its heels. His tyres screeched and skidded. He flipped the steering wheel one way and then the other, fighting to keep it on the track, allowing the gold car to pull away from him. The spectators *oohed* and *aahed*. Had Herbert lost control? Was it all going to end in disaster because of his determination to win? Thankfully, he quickly corrected his error and was driving in a straight line again, much to the crowd's approval. The garage breathed a collective sigh of relief, as did Jack.

'Now watch him go,' said Patrick. The smile on his face told Jack everything. Herbert was going to attack.

And he did.

The drivers reached the corner at the end of the home straight and Herbert was right behind the gold car. Then, to everyone's surprise – and the crowd's excitement – he overtook on the outside. Jack cupped his hands over his mouth and nose, peeping over the top of them; even he knew

Herbert was taking a big risk with this dangerous manoeuvre. But in a flash, Herbert was past him and up into fifth. The cars disappeared and Jack had to wait for almost two minutes for them to return.

The screaming lady, from earlier, was running her hands through her hair and puffing out her cheeks.

The noise was building again. The black number 20 was now in front, the yellow number 4 was second and the two green cars were third and fourth, with Herbert right behind them.

The race was entering the final three laps, but Herbert was still fifth. Once again, they flew around the final corner and there was only a paper's width between Herbert and the car in front. As soon as they exited the bend, he moved out and effortlessly went past the next driver. The crowd were on their feet and the garage was going wild; he was almost there – just a couple more laps.

'Herbie! Herbie! Herbie!' echoed around the stands.

The team managers were now at the front. The mechanics, Herbert's friends and the crowd were all shouting, egging him on and willing him to victory. Jack, hands cupped over his mouth, glanced up at Patrick, who was intently watching the final moments of the race unfold.

The cars disappeared, but the crowd continued chanting. Previously, they'd only sounded their encouragement whenever the cars came into view and attacked the home straight, but now it was continuous, as if their support would carry all the way around the track and push Herbert to the chequered flag.

The cars were coming around quicker and quicker. The black number 20 was still in the lead, closely followed by the green number 6, and there, right behind them, was Herbert! He was flying, taking the zig-zagging corners, skidding around and straightening, all in one movement.

The cars hit the home straight and Jack waved like crazy, hoping his grandad would see him as he sped past, but he was far too busy hunting down the car in front. The cars flew around the corner and were, once again, out of sight.

'He's gonna make it!' said Jack.

Patrick said, 'Not yet. There are still two laps remaining ... that's twenty-eight corners, anything can happen. One false move, one collision, a puncture, a poor exit from a corner – there are so many things that can go wrong.'

'He will make it, though, won't he?'

'We'll soon find out. He's by far the best driver out there. So, failing a mechanical problem, he should hold on. Remember, he needs to beat number 20, the black car.'

'But the black car's ahead of him!'

Patrick nodded. 'It's going to be close.'

Jack's eyes were drawn to his left again. The lady was jumping up and down and yelling, 'Go, Herbie, go!'

Jack slid along the barrier towards her. Patrick didn't notice: his eyes wouldn't leave the track. Jack sidled up next to the lady. He didn't say a word, he just turned to the track and watched.

The roar returned, and it was even more fierce. The intense atmosphere inside the garage was electric. The mechanics and the pit crew crowded the wall. Managers were craning their necks to see what was going on. There was nothing more they could do now. It was all down to Herbert. It was too much for one mechanic: he remained at the back of the garage with his head in his hands.

This was it. After two hours of solid driving, the drivers rounded the last few bends before attacking the final lap. The last fourteen corners. The last two minutes of a gruelling race. The end of a brutal season-long battle to become world champion!

The black car came flying around the corner. Jack threw his hands up to his face, fingers splayed. This was getting too much. Was it over? Or was Herbert close enough to battle for the win on the final lap? Time stood still. But then another car came sweeping around the bend. It was five metres behind the leader, but the flash of red made Jack and the whole garage explode with excitement. It was Herbert! He was now up in second position. A ferocious roar exploded as everyone – even the guy who, moments earlier, had been at the back of the garage with his head in his hands – rushed over to the railings, getting as close to the track as possible. Jack felt himself being crushed in the surge.

'Hey, be careful! There's a boy down here,' came a protective-sounding voice.

Jack looked up and recognised the lady who'd been screaming for his grandad to 'push it!' moments earlier.

'Are you okay, little man?' she asked.

Jack nodded and flung his arms over the railings and looked to the right. Union Jack flags were swirling around, people were jumping up and down, willing Herbert to victory. The noise built for one final time. One final lap. One final push. Hands were in front of faces. Some people looked like they were praying or even crying.

The cars approached and Patrick's hands were, once again, braced on top of his head, his cheeks puffed out like a hamster. Jack's eyes were fixed, unblinking, on the corner. He was desperate to see a flash of red. But he didn't. His heart sank when he saw the black car fly around the corner for the last time.

Jack cradled his head. It was all over, he thought. His grandad had come so close, but it wasn't enough. However, the crowd let Jack know it wasn't over, not yet; they were still jumping up and down, waving their flags and sounding horns.

As the black car straightened up, there, right next to it, attacking on the outside, was a burst of red ... It was Herbert! Patrick joined the crowd in yelling and jumping around; his face was as red as Herbert's helmet.

The cars rounded the final corner, wheel to wheel, pushing each other to the finish line to take the win and, ultimately, the championship. The whole garage was bouncing up and down, shouting and screaming, desperate for their number one driver to become world champion.

'Come on, Herbie! Go!' shouted the lady next to Jack, banging the railings with her hands.

Jack jumped up and down. 'Go, Grandad, go!' He didn't care if anyone heard him, there was only one thing that mattered now: pushing his grandad home to win the race and become world champion.

The cars were neck and neck and their wheels touched, forcing a plume of smoke into the atmosphere. More *oohs* and *ahhs* exploded from the crowd.

At the finish line, the race controller gripped the chequered flag, waiting for the winner to claim their prize. They were eighty metres from the finish line with no clear winner. Jack wasn't sure how much more he could take, the atmosphere was so tense!

Jack screamed, 'Come on Grandad, pull your finger out!'

By now, everyone was hanging over the railings. The pit crew and the mechanics shouting as loudly as they could; just like Jack, they were desperate for the win.

With only forty metres to go, Herbert edged in front. The crowd exploded, giving it everything they had. He was nearly there, but his rival wasn't giving up and he inched back alongside. There were centimetres between their wheels. It was nail-biting stuff.

Jack brought his hands up to his face and watched the final seconds through splayed fingers. With only fifteen metres to go, Herbert gave one final push, edging mere inches ahead just before crossing the line and claiming the chequered flag. He'd done it! The garage erupted, the crowd exploded, the lady next to Jack was in tears.

Patrick ran over, threw his arms around Jack and lifted him from the ground in celebration. Everyone in the garage was beaming and giving each other congratulatory back-slaps and hugs as if they'd driven the car themselves. Patrick released Jack, but he was immediately grabbed by the lady next to him. She bent down and wrapped her arms around him. Her tear-stained face rubbed against his cheek. Not that he cared, she smelt so good. Jack flung his arms around her neck and squeezed her tight.

'He did it! He really did it!' she said, releasing Jack and kissing him on the cheek as the tears flowed.

Jack was so happy. The pride he felt for his grandad was like nothing he'd ever felt before. The crowd, the garage, his friends and, undoubtedly the nation, had all been hoping for the win. It had all rested on his grandad's broad shoulders, and he had delivered.

People everywhere were hugging each other and flags were being waved enthusiastically. Men and women were dancing and bouncing around with tears of joy streaming down their faces.

Tears also prickled Jack's eyes. He raised his hands and wiped them away; they were the happiest tears he'd ever cried. He couldn't wait to see his grandad and give him the biggest hug. And now, Jack knew what he wanted to be when he was older. He wanted to be a famous racing driver and become world champion.

Just like his grandad.

CHAPTER TWENTY-SIX

Grandad!

With the drivers completing a lap of honour and thanking the fans for their support, Patrick placed his hands on Jack's shoulders. 'Well, what did you think of that?'

'It was amazing. He did it! He's World Champion!' said Jack, bursting with pride.

'He is ... I was so engrossed in the race I didn't see you slide over here. Good job I didn't lose you.'

'I won't tell Herbie if you don't,' joked Jack. 'Anyway, this nice lady looked after me.'

Patrick smiled at the woman. She flung her arms around him, squeezed him tight, and kissed him on the cheek. 'He did it. He really did it!'

After their embrace, Patrick placed his hand on the top of Jack's head. 'This little man is Jack, he's a friend of Herbie's.'

She held out her hand. 'Well, it's a pleasure to meet you, Jack. Did you enjoy the race?'

'Too right,' he said, smiling away. 'It was brilliant!'

'I'm sorry if I crushed you, I was a little excited, that's all.'

'It's okay. I'm a strong boy.'

'Indeed, you are. Anyway, no doubt I'll see you later ...'

Jack smiled and nodded. 'I certainly hope so.'

She bent down, kissed him on the cheek and walked over to her friends.

Patrick said, 'Right, Jack. Let's get over and watch the presentation, shall we?'

They made their way through the pit crew, the reporters and the fans to get to the podium.

Eventually, the cars came to a standstill and the drivers climbed out. Jack watched his grandad jump out of his car, remove his dirty goggles, and look round. A wreath was immediately placed around his neck, and he was passed a magnum of champagne. He spotted Jack, raised the bottle in his grandson's direction, and winked. Jack giggled and gave a double thumbs up.

Herbert, along with the drivers finishing in second and third, climbed onto the podium to take their congratulations. Fresh chants of 'Herbie! Herbie! Herbie!' filled the air. Their champion turned and saluted his fans, leading to yet more cheering and chanting. The three drivers then drank champagne from the bottles.

His grandad had always been Jack's hero. In fact, he didn't even have to do anything to be his hero. It didn't matter if he'd been a bin-man, a bus driver, or a coal worker when he was younger: Jack loved him no matter what. The fact he was a world champion racing driver? Well, that was a bonus!

With the ceremony completed, Herbert made his way over to Jack and Patrick, accepting hugs and congratulatory smacks on the back along the way. So many people wanted to talk to him and ask questions, which he obliged in doing, although his eyes never wavered from Jack. It was as if they were having a full-on conversation without either of them saying a word.

Herbert finally fought his way through the crowd, bent down, and looked into his grandson's adoring eyes. 'Well?'

Jack broke into the biggest smile, flung his arms around Herbert's neck and squeezed him tighter than he ever had before. 'I never needed a reason for you to be my hero, but now I have one, anyway. I love you, Grandad.'

'I love you too, Jack, my boy.'

'Excuse me,' came a voice from behind. 'Is there any chance of you sharing that affection, *Mr World Champion?*'

It was the sweet-smelling lady who had, earlier, saved Jack from being crushed. She stepped forward, threw her arms around Herbert and gave him a smacker, right on the lips! Jack's eyes almost popped out of his head. In fact, he had to look away.

'I'm so proud of you,' she said, squeezing Herbert ever tighter.

'Thank you,' said Herbert, smiling and giving her a hug. 'Have you met Jack?'

'Yes, we met earlier. Hello again,' she said, leaving her arm slung around Herbert's shoulder.

'Hi,' said Jack.

'Jack, this is my girlfriend, Jean.'

Without thinking, Jack blurted out, 'Grandma?'

Jean huffed, but then giggled. 'Well, that's charming. Do I look that old? Maybe I need a facelift?'

'No .... Sorry ... My grandma's called Jean, that's all!'

'Well, your grandma must be really cool, because Jean is an awesome name.'

'Yeah, she is ... So's my grandad.'

Herbert winked at Jack.

'Anyway, I'll meet you once you've had a shower,' said Jean.

Herbert nodded and gave his girlfriend another kiss. This time, Jack didn't look away, he smiled.

'Bye, Jack. It was so nice to meet you.'

'You, too.'

And with that, his twenty-one-year-old grandma disappeared into the crowd.

'Right, let's go,' said Herbert, grabbing Jack by the hand and heading towards the exit.

Working through the crowd was a struggle. Everyone wanted to ask questions, have photographs taken with the new world champion, or, simply, offer their congratulations.

They continued to move forward with Herbert's strong hand tightly wrapped around Jack's. But it was no use, people were swarming all around, crowding Herbert, firing question after question at him. They needed to escape, and there was only one way that was going to be possible. Herbert reached down with his free hand and twisted the button on the time-traveller's watch.

Suddenly, the strong, youthful hand wrapped around Jack's own, became weak and withered, the grip eased and, as they walked through the main entrance into the setting sun, Jack's skin began to tingle.

He closed his eyes and shook his head as the voices around him became muffled. When he next opened them, people were walking right through them. Jack and Herbert had, once again, become invisible.

Herbert turned to look at Jack. A faint smile lingered there, but his eyes looked tired. Herbert's hand went to his face, and he stumbled.

'Grandad!' Jack cried out, alarmed. He moved up beside Herbert and grabbed him around the waist.

'It's okay ... I'm okay. But we need to get home.'

When they reached the time machine, Jack opened the door and helped his grandad into his seat. He looked pale, like he might pass out at any moment.

'Jack, it's down to you to get us home. Can you remember how to do it?' mumbled Herbert through shallow breaths.

'Are you going to be okay, Grandad?'

Herbert gave a weak smile. 'I'm going to be fine, but you need to get us home. Can you do it?'

Jack was unsure. He'd never done it all by himself before. He was nervous and afraid. But then he remembered what he had just seen his grandad do and drew strength from it.

'I can.'

'Good boy, Jack. Good boy ...' said Herbert, sounding like he was about to drift off to sleep.

Jack knew he had to get them home, and fast. He set the digital display to the correct date and adjusted the dials. He strapped his grandad in and wiped the sweat from his brow. Herbert was panting and struggling to stay awake.

Jack touched Herbert's hand. 'You're going to be okay, Grandad. I'll get us home.'

Herbert didn't reply. Jack strapped himself in and pressed the glowing launch button.

Moments later, they exploded from underground and soared through a cloudless, darkening sky, heading back home. Jack didn't look out of the window, nor did he continually check the display. He listened to the beeping alarms, which would let him know if there was something to worry about. He gave the display the odd glance, now and then, to ensure all was as it should be. Other than that, Jack's eyes never wavered from his grandad; not once, during the entire journey.

Deep down, Jack knew this would be their last trip together ... not that it mattered. All he cared about was getting them back safely. The trips had now become completely irrelevant.

Jack sat in silence and watched his grandad as he slept. He hoped he'd have a chance to ask the many questions spinning around inside his head. Only time would tell.

2012

CHAPTER TWENTY-SEVEN

Back Home

Herbert slept for the entire journey back. With the time machine shut down, Jack let his grandad continue to get some well-earned rest. It'd never occurred to Jack that their adventures would come to an end so abruptly, but they had. If he had any doubts before, he was certain now. Seeing his grandad so tired – much more than normal – made him realise he couldn't put him through it again.

Twenty minutes later, Jack climbed from his seat and shut down the display. He placed a hand on his grandad's shoulder, and gently rocked him awake. 'Grandad, we're home.'

Herbert stirred, and then his eyes blinked open. He brought his hands up and gently rubbed them over his face. He stretched and opened his eyes to see Jack standing over him, a half-smile on his face. 'You got us home, my boy. I'm so proud of you,' he said, patting Jack on the arm.

'Are you okay?'

Herbert gave a weak smile. 'I'm fine, Jack. I think I may have overdone it today, but I'm fine ...'

Jack nodded and settled back into his seat, giving his grandad time to completely wake from his slumber.

'Any problems on the way back?'

Jack shook his head. 'None.'

'That's good. You're such a clever boy. Any sweets left?'

Jack reached into his bag and pulled out a pack of mints. 'Here you go.'

As Herbert enjoyed the sweets, Jack tidied everything away and made sure the machine was left clean and tidy.

'Better, Grandad?' asked Jack.

'Much better, thanks. I guess I'm at that age where I need to be looked after,' he smiled. 'Just not by my 11-year-old grandson!'

Jack sat with his bag between his legs. 'You were amazing today, Grandad.'

'Did you enjoy the race?' Herbert asked, perking up and sitting straight in his seat.

'I loved it. I never knew you used to be a racing driver ... mum and dad never told me.'

'Ah,' Herbert said, raising a finger in the air, 'that's because your grandma wouldn't allow it. She doesn't like to talk about it too much.' His grandad leant closer. 'She likes to think she's the special one in this family.'

Jack laughed. 'She is. You both are!'

'Well, it was a long time ago, but it was a huge part of my life. I'm sorry I didn't tell you about it, or that I would be transforming into my younger self. You see, I didn't want to ruin the surprise. It was one of the best days of my life and I wanted you to experience it properly. Y'know, smell the oil, mix with the crowd, be part of the garage team. Be there for real.'

'And meet grandma,' smiled Jack.

'That too. The thing is, I wanted you to see I'm not just the silly old man you see every week. I wanted to show you what I used to be. Back in the day.'

'I'll always see you as a *silly old man*,' Jack joked. 'But you're meant to be like that; you're my grandad and I wouldn't have you any other way.'

Herbert smiled and stood up. He cupped Jack's face with his hands. 'You're the most precious, loving, caring grandson I could have ever wished for. I'm the luckiest grandad in the world.'

Herbert wrapped his arms around Jack and kissed the top of his head.

Jack said, 'You're not as lucky as me.'

'Why's that?' asked Herbert.

Jack giggled. 'Because I have the best grandma in the world.'

'Charming!'

'I guess you're okay, as well, Grandad.'

'Anyway, speaking of your grandma,' Herbert said, 'we'd best get inside; she'll be back soon, and I need to make it look like I've at least attempted to do some housework.'

Jack nodded and helped his grandad through the door. Herbert stretched before leading Jack past the old racing car in the middle of his garage. Jack stopped and rubbed his hand over the faded gold lettering at the back. He kept his hand on the car and caressed it as he walked towards the front. It looked tired now. Jack reached the front and saw the faint outline of a circle. It was covered in dust and grime. Herbert turned and lovingly watched Jack place his right hand on the edge of the circle.

'Hold on,' said Herbert. He grabbed a cloth from the bench and threw it over. 'Try that.'

Jack rubbed the cloth over the circle, revealing a black '10'. He traced his finger over the digits. Herbert watched with satisfaction: the seed had been planted.

Jack had a thought. He walked to the rear of the car and stopped at the gold lettering. He gently rubbed away with the cloth, but it was so faded that the only thing he could make out was an outline of two letters: 'H' followed by 'E'.

Jack turned to look at his grandad. 'Herbie,' he said, smiling.

Herbert shook his head, reached under the bench and removed an old shoebox. He beckoned Jack over and lifted the lid. It contained medals, ribbons, magazine cuttings, and newspaper articles. Herbert removed an old newspaper cutting and passed it to Jack, who read the headline aloud: 'Hellraiser wins World Championship.' The article was from the race Jack had just witnessed.

'*Hellraiser*? Was that your nickname?'

Herbert nodded. 'It was. I had a bit of a reputation in my younger days. The name was used in an early article and it stuck with me from that moment on.'

'I like it. It makes you sound like a troublemaker!'

'I was!'

They leant against the bench, staring at the racing car in silence.

'She's a bit battered now,' admitted Herbert.

Jack said without hesitation, 'She's perfect.'

'I'm glad you like her, because, when you're old enough, she's all yours.'

'Really?' gasped Jack.

Herbert nodded. 'If you want her that is?'

'Of course I do!' Jack said, flinging his arms around Herbert's waist. 'Thank you, Grandad!'

'Good,' Herbert said, hugging him back. 'Or she'd have ended up on the scrap heap.'

'What? No way! I'm going to keep her and I'm going to learn how to repair her. She'll look as good as she used to.'

'I'm sure you'll look after her just fine, my boy.'

'Grandad?' asked Jack.

'Yes?'

'Did you always want to be a racing driver? I mean, before you spent that day at Mr Hucklebuck's house?'

'I didn't know what I wanted to be, or what I wanted to do when I left school. But once I spent time at that garage, it hit me. I knew, there and then, what I wanted to be. The excitement I felt was indescribable. I had the biggest rush, my skin was tingling and my heart was racing.'

Jack nodded.

'The thing is, Jack, you need to know what you want from life. You may not know now. You may not know when you leave school. You may not even know when you start your first job. But, one day, when you least expect it, something will happen, and you'll get the biggest rush. The key thing to remember is to go for it, whatever it is. Don't let anybody tell you it's impossible, or to stop dreaming. If it's meant to happen, it will. If you have a passion for something, if it excites you and gives you the biggest thrill whenever you imagine yourself doing it, then go for it. Remember, it's always better to try something and not succeed than to not try and always wonder *what if.* Understand?'

Jack thought for a moment. 'I understand, Grandad.'

'Good boy. Right, let's go up,' said Herbert and headed for the door.

'I already know what I want to be,' Jack said, not taking his eyes from the battered old car that had carried his grandad to the 1962 world championship.

'Really?'

Jack nodded. 'I want to be a racing driver. I want to be like my hero. I want to be just like you.'

Herbert felt tears prickle his eyes. He blinked them away and smiled. 'That's my boy, Jack.'

He ruffled Jack's hair before stepping outside.

'Grandad?'

Herbert turned back. 'Yes?'

'Did you want to go back today for your benefit, or mine?'

'Both,' replied Herbert and winked.

Herbert headed up the path, leaving Jack to have some time alone with the racing car he would own when he was old enough. He stepped into the kitchen and sighed, realising he had one last thing to do today: as much housework as possible before his wife came home and grilled him, once again, for being lazy and doing nothing all afternoon.

CHAPTER TWENTY-EIGHT

The Last Trip

Jack stayed for the rest of the afternoon and helped tidy up. It was the least he could do after the amazing adventure his grandad had taken him on. Before long, the keys jingled in the lock and in walked Jean and Ethel.

Herbert turned off the hoover he was pushing along the carpet, ran over, and gave his wife a bear hug. 'Hello, beautiful, how was your day?'

Jean stood with her arms pinned to her sides, while her best friend screwed her face up and shook her head at the revolting sight.

'What are you doing, Herbie?' spat Jean.

'Just giving you a hug. Is that not allowed?'

Jack laughed, while Ethel continued to show her displeasure by tutting, very loudly.

Jean wriggled free. 'Get off me, you buffoon.'

Jack had an idea. 'Hey, is there any chance of me getting some of that affection?'

Herbert jolted, his eyes dancing as he rubbed the back of his neck. Jean said nothing, but she looked at Jack and gave a wry smile. 'What does he mean, Herbie?'

'Erm ...' said a nervous Herbert. 'Oh, he just wants a hug from his grandma.'

The room fell silent. There was no need for either of them to say anything. Jack had uttered the same phrase his grandma had used back in 1962; words she'd said to his grandad right after the race, all those years ago.

'Well, are we going to stand out here all day, or are you going to get the kettle on, Herbie?' snapped Ethel.

'Of course. Would you like that to go?' asked Herbert, looking over his wife's shoulder at her grumpy friend.

Jean lifted the hand resting on Herbert's shoulder and slapped him on the arm. 'Don't be so rude,' she said and then did something Jack had not seen for a long time. She leant in and kissed her husband on the cheek. Jack caught the look between them: pure love and affection.

Herbert winked and, as Jean edged past, he reached one hand down and squeezed her bum, making her shriek. 'Oops,' he said. 'Sorry, my hand slipped!'

Jean said nothing. Instead, she reached behind and pinched her husband's bum, making him giggle like a schoolboy.

'Well, come on in, Ethel. I'm not paying to warm the outside world, you know. Unless, of course, you want to shoot home to see how your neighbour's doing?' joked Herbert, which caused Jack to laugh.

'No, I'm not going home.'

'Shame,' mumbled Herbert.

'I want a cup of tea first. We only had one in town and it tasted disgusting,' she said, shuffling past him. He didn't pinch her bum; instead, he moved away with a look of horror on his face, jokingly fending her off with his index fingers made into the sign of a cross.

'Only because she had to blinkin' pay for it,' whispered Herbert to his grandson.

Jack covered his mouth with both hands to keep his laughter in check, and then headed into the sitting room, closely followed by his grandad.

They sat opposite each other, not knowing how to start the conversation neither of them wanted. Herbert picked up his newspaper and began flicking through it, not settling on one page for long enough to take anything in. He occasionally looked over the top of the paper, meeting his grandson's eye, who was doing likewise with his comic.

Eventually, Jack reached into his bag and removed William Bertrand's letter. He walked over to his grandad and passed it back to him.

'Oh, thanks,' whispered Herbert, hurriedly stuffing it down the side of his chair. 'Did it make sense?'

'Perfect sense.' Jack paused for a second. 'Was that what made you weaker than normal today, Grandad? I mean, transferring into your younger self?'

Herbert smiled and pulled Jack onto the arm of his chair. 'I'm getting old, Jack. Everything is harder when you get to my age. And even if the time travelling does drain a bit of my energy, well, I wouldn't change a thing. We've had so much fun and created the best memories over the years, and I couldn't think of a better way to spend my free time than to go travelling with you. I'm surprised you still want to hang around with an old fossil like me.'

Jack wrapped his arms around Herbert's neck. 'I couldn't think of anything better, but that was our last trip, wasn't it, Grandad?'

Herbert pulled Jack away from him. 'I'm not saying we'll never go again, Jack, but, like I said, each time we travel it takes a lot longer for me to recover.'

Jack nodded. 'I know.'

'It doesn't mean it has to stop completely. We just need to choose our trips more carefully.'

Jack shook his head. 'No. It stops.'

'Jack, I don't want you to miss out.'

'And I don't want to put you through anything like that again. I would rather have ten more years of sitting here with you, chatting, laughing and winding up grandma, than three more years travelling back in time to see things I can get from the internet. I can't go online and get another one of you, can I?'

Herbert raised his hand and lovingly stroked Jack's head. 'You're the most precious thing in the world to me, and we'll do whatever you want. If it's to wind up your grandma, well, I think we can manage that!'

'Great,' smiled Jack.

'Jean!' shouted Herbert, winking.

The serving hatch above Herbert's head, flew open, revealing a disgruntled Jean. 'What?'

'Jack was asking if he could stay for tea?'

'Of course he can stay for tea! What sort of a silly question is that?'

'Good. That means I can take him down the pub for a lemonade while you're cooking. There's better company down there anyway, and the women adore me. Not that I can blame them …'

An orange came flying through the hatch and hit Herbert on the head.

'Idiot,' muttered Jean.

Jack and Herbert laughed at the sound of the hatch being slammed shut behind them.

'You really are going to be in so much trouble when I go, Grandad.'

'It's the only way to live, Jack.'

Half an hour later, with Ethel marching down the road and heading back home, Jack escaped his grandma's clutches and pulled his coat from the hook. Herbert stood with his hands in his pockets and waited for Jack to slip his coat on, while Jean shuffled her way back to the kitchen, leaving her husband and her grandson to say their goodbyes.

'Thanks, Grandad. That was such an amazing day.'

'It was, wasn't it?'

'The best. I'm so proud of you. I never dreamt you were such a big hit when you were younger.'

Herbert stood proud. 'What do you mean when I was *younger*? I'm still a big hit, especially with the ladies.'

Jack rolled his eyes, although he was smiling. 'I'll see you next week?'

'What? You can't leave me alone with her for that long!' laughed Herbert, throwing his head towards the kitchen. 'I need a break at some point or one of us won't make it to the weekend.'

Jack threw his arms around his grandad, who responded and hugged Jack tighter than ever.

'Thanks, Grandad ... for everything.'

'You're welcome. Now, be careful on that death-trap and make sure your mum texts your grandma once you're home.'

Herbert kissed the top of Jack's head, watched him climb on his bike and disappear around the corner. He closed the door and headed towards the kitchen, where Jean was standing with her back to the sink, drying her hands.

'How was your day with moaning Ethel?' asked Herbert, leaning against the doorframe with his hands in his pockets.

'That's not what you normally ask me.'

'Oh well, just being nice ...'

'You look tired. Everything alright?'

'Everything's fantastic,' beamed Herbert.

'How was he?'

Herbert laughed and shook his head. 'Like a grown up. That boy melts my heart every day.'

'I know, me too. He's like his mother.'

'And his grandmother,' added Herbert. He walked over, wrapped his arms around his wife, and kissed her gently on the forehead.

'About time you gave me some of that affection, Herbert Finch,' she said and giggled.

'So, Mrs Finch, what shall we do this afternoon?'

'Well, what do you want to do?' Jean asked, nestling against Herbert's chest.

'How do you fancy having some fun?'

'Why, Herbert, I thought you'd never ask,' she said, raising her head and kissing him on the cheek. 'But, looking at the state of you, I'm driving this time.'

He threw his hands up and conceded. 'Fair enough.'

Jean and Herbert headed out of the back door and down the path to the garage. Herbert opened the creaky wooden door and let his wife in first. The smell of oil, sawdust, and old tins of paint filled their nostrils. They crunched their way over the wood shavings and stopped at the once bright red racing car, both tapping the '10' that was now clearly visible. They eased their way down the side of the car until they reached the rear. Jean placed an index finger on the gold letter H, Herbert placed his on top. They traced their fingers over the two remaining letters – remembering the significance of them. Herbert kissed his wife on the cheek, then walked to the back of the garage and grabbed the large green sheet. There was a loud *swoosh* as he pulled it back to reveal the solid black door of the time machine. After entering the code, Herbert popped the door open and stepped to the side, again, allowing Jean to walk in first. Herbert followed his wife and locked the door behind them.

Ten minutes later, Jean and Herbert Finch were soaring high above the clouds and travelling back in time to relive one of their most treasured memories together of years gone by.

2022

CHAPTER TWENTY-NINE

New Legacy

Jack waited in his trailer. A stereo played in the background; something he used to help calm his nerves, but, today, it wasn't working. His heart was racing, his palms were sweaty, and his mouth was dry. This was the moment. After all the hard work. The hours and hours of practice. The time spent on the road away from his family and loved ones. He'd put his heart into making this, his dream, come true. And now he was here, waiting to head out. The final journey of the past ten years.

It had all started a week after that final trip in the time machine, when Jack had seen his grandad crowned world champion. They'd visited the local karting track and, from the first corner, Jack was fanatical. He understood what the thrill of racing meant and why his grandad and Mr Hucklebuck loved it so much. After a month, Jack entered local competitions and, within a year, reached the regional finals. Two years after that, he was in the nationals. He continued to rise through the rankings, and it wasn't long before the big teams were showing a keen interest in him. When Jack turned eighteen, they all came calling. His family connection was enough to make people sit up and take notice, but the question remained: was Jack as good as his grandad? He answered it emphatically by winning with ease most weeks. He was smooth, majestic, but above all else, he proved to be a natural.

It'd been an amazing journey, and Herbert had been with him every step of the way. That was, until he passed away, just three years ago. Losing his grandad hit Jack like a ton of bricks. He came close to giving up. In fact, he may well have if it hadn't been for his grandma. She'd reasoned with him, encouraged him and showed compassion. Finally, when none of that helped, the Finch finger came out and Jack was told in no uncertain terms what she thought.

'Now, look here, Jack. Your grandad loved you more than anything. He took you karting every week, even when he wasn't feeling well. The silly old sausage even stood out in the cold, the rain, and the blazing sunshine – coming home some weeks and going straight to bed. But he didn't do it for himself, he did it for you. You were all he cared about. And now you have a chance to repay him. He's up there watching you,' she added, pointing her index finger skywards. 'He never let you down, so don't you let him down! Not now. Not when it really matters. Understood?'

Jack went to respond but stopped when he saw the look on his grandma's face. There was no point. She'd spoken, and that was the end of the matter. Jack wouldn't be allowed to give up. His grandad was good at being funny and playing for laughs, and this was what his grandma was good at: tough love. And it worked every single time.

Jack took a deep breath, stood, and pulled up his overalls. He turned on the tap and splashed cold water on his face, letting it roll down his long, broad nose before landing with the loudest *plink*. He closed his eyes and took another deep breath.

A knock on the door startled him. He grabbed a towel and wiped his face as the door opened.

'How are you feeling?' asked his grandma.

Jack puffed out his cheeks, dropped the towel and ran his fingers through his hair.

'Hey, don't worry, it'll be fine once you're out there,' added Jean with a sympathetic smile. 'You know why you're here. You've worked so hard. You've earned this.'

Jack nodded, walked over to the sofa, and sat down. Jean walked over and sat down next to him, placing a caring hand on his knee. 'He'd be so proud of you,' she said, nodding at the photograph of Herbert, in pride of place on the wall. 'And you're going to do him and yourself proud today. No matter what happens.'

She kissed Jack on the cheek and stood to leave.

'I hope you're right. Thank you for always being here for me.'

'What are grandmas for?' asked Jean, before nodding at the photograph again. 'He's here too, you know.'

Jack smiled and nodded. 'I know.'

Jean winked and headed outside to join Jack's mum and dad, who were in the main stand waiting to watch Jack's first race of the season, together.

Jack looked around at the racing photographs and memorabilia scattered across the walls of his trailer. There were reports on his rise through the rankings, his performances in the lower classed events, and numerous newspaper articles. And right there, front and centre, the photograph his grandma had pointed out. A man in white overalls was sitting in the seat of an old racing car, holding a gold trophy aloft with one hand while the other was clutching a magnum of champagne. There was a huge wreath around his neck and the biggest smile displayed on his soot-covered face. The headline of the article was one Jack had kept close to his heart for many years. 'Hellraiser wins World Championship.' He stared at it for what seemed like forever, somehow gaining motivation from it.

Jack kissed his fingers and touched his grandad's face. 'Help me like you always used to, Grandad ...'

His gaze fell on another photograph next to the article. Jack was sitting in a racing car that had once looked like nothing more than a pile of scrap metal, left abandoned in his grandad's garage. It was now back to its former glory: fire-engine red, with a glistening chrome exhaust pipe. A crisp white circle was sitting at the front, with a jet-black '10' centred inside it. It'd taken Jack four years to restore his grandad's winning car from 1962, but it had been worth the effort.

Jack popped on his sunglasses and stepped outside to a flurry of flashing lightbulbs. People were running around with headsets on, disappearing into trailers and talking to team members. Reporters rushed over and thrust microphones in his face; cameras continued to flash, bathing Jack in the brightest light as they tried to get that headline picture.

Fans came rushing over, attempting to get a last-minute autograph. Jack wasn't keen on this sort of attention – this wasn't what he'd signed up for – but he was the rising star, the grandson of the famous Herbert Finch. Nobody could believe the talent Jack had. But he was bound to be good with Finch blood running through his veins.

He reached the pit lane and headed towards his garage. They were all ready and waiting for him. More reporters and TV crews were present, all wrapped up in the excited buzz. Jack removed his sunglasses and came to a stop right in front of the car. People were coming up to talk to him, but one simple gesture told them to back away. A solitary finger raised and pointed at all of them. The finger he'd received countless times from his grandma when he was younger: her signal, warning you to not push your luck. It always worked, especially when accompanied by a scowl. Although, Jack's gesture was different. It was a clear signal: stay back; this is a private moment. Everyone obeyed, standing motionless, as if hypnotised.

Jack placed his hand on the front of the car and double-tapped the number '10'. He worked his way towards the rear, his hand caressing the logos of the sponsors. He stopped at the rear wing and traced the gold lettering with his index finger and smiled. Everyone knew what that lettering meant to Jack; he'd made no bones about the importance of the three small but very significant words. They meant so much to him.

He brought his hand to his lips, kissed his fingers, and gave the lettering a double tap before moving around the rest of the car. He took his helmet from a mechanic standing at the front. Jack completed his pre-race checks and rolled out of the garage.

As he trundled around the track, his mind wandered. He imagined his grandad standing on every corner. His favourite newsboy cap sitting proudly on top of his head as he smiled and waved in encouragement. Herbert had never missed a single one of Jack's karting races. He was always there to offer a consoling hug on a bad day, or a congratulatory thumbs up and comment like 'that's my boy' when Jack had been victorious. It never mattered where Jack finished because, in his grandad's eyes, he was always a winner. Herbert had supported Jack through everything, and now it was his turn.

Jack weaved his way around the track and headed down the finishing straight. The cars completed their formation lap and lined up on the starting grid, engines revving; animals waiting to be released from their traps. Jack patiently waited as, one-by-one, the starting lights illuminated. He took a deep breath and puffed out his cheeks, foot revving the engine, hands gripping the wheel. He knew inside the gloves his knuckles would be white. Cars lined up in front of him, stretching all the way to the five red lights hanging ominously over the start-finish line. His heart was pounding like never before; he was sure it was going to burst out of his chest. He focused on the lights, shutting everything else out. They were all that mattered now. They came rushing towards him.

This was it.

His right foot gently pumped the accelerator: two quick pulses, then a third longer press. The engine roared its approval, confirming it was ready. Jack loosened his grip, allowing the blood to rush to his knuckles. His eyes narrowed. He was set. The lights disappeared, and he floored it.

The roar of the engines filled the circuit with the most deafening noise. The crowd went wild.

Burning rubber, mixed with the smoke hanging in the air, filled his nostrils, fuelling the adrenaline pumping around his body. By the time they reached the first corner, Jack was already gaining on the cars in front. He braked, changed gear, and made his way around the outside, snaking through a series of bends before hitting the long straight at the rear of the track. He accelerated again and shot past the highly-polished black car in front. His engine was purring with every slight adjustment to his racing line.

He shifted gear again.

The car roared its approval.

His heart raced faster.

Jack was flying.

And then, as his heart rate reduced, Jack took a deep breath. He felt the blood coursing through his veins and, for the first time that day, he relaxed. This was what he was born to do. He could hear the calming voice of his grandad in his ear, 'Come on, Jack, my boy. You can do this.'

Jack shifted gear and weaved his way between two more cars. The crowd erupted. He slowed for the next corner and caught sight of a banner that simply read, 'Go, Jack, Go!'

Jack smiled. 'This one's for you, Grandad.'

He exited the corner, changed gear and depressed the accelerator. The car responded and shot forwards.

As Jack sped past another car, he imagined the gold lettering making up the three words on his rear wing begin to glow. Soon, just like the racing car in the newspaper article from 1962, *Herbie the Hellraiser* was zooming past cars on his way to another victory.

NINE MONTHS LATER

CHAPTER THIRTY

The Season Finale

Jack was world champion. In his first season. It was unheard of but he'd had the driving force of Herbert behind him. It was all he'd ever wanted – to emulate his grandad, and now he had achieved that. Things could have been so different if his mum had stopped him from going to that very first karting session. But she hadn't, thanks to some gentle persuasion from Herbert.

After winning the world championship, there was only one thing Jack wanted to do: to see his grandad. He smiled through interviews, and answered every question from the reporters, before being swamped by his team and family, all hugging him and giving celebratory slaps on the back.

Finally, he fell into his grandma's outstretched arms. Tears filled her eyes as she drew him to her, for the tightest of hugs.

'He would be so proud of you,' she said, her voice cracking. 'Just as I am.'

Jack hugged her tighter. His grandma kissed him on the cheek and whispered something in his ear that made him freeze. 'Go.'

Jack frowned and pulled away. '*Go*? Go where?'

'You know where.'

As he looked into the loving eyes of his grandma, the realisation hit him. 'You mean, you know about the time machine? Since when?'

'Jack,' she said, cupping his face in her wrinkled hands. 'I've always known.' She gave him a wink. 'Now, go ...'

'Come with me,' pleaded Jack.

Jean shook her head. 'Next time. This is your moment. After all, you're his boy.'

Jack pulled her to him for one final hug, kissed her on the forehead, and then he was gone.

Jack headed straight for the time machine. He'd used it on so many occasions to do the one thing he loved more than anything: to watch his grandad race. He'd seen every single event, using what he learnt from them to replicate Herbert's racing style. Everyone thought driving the way Jack did was in his blood. Professionals always remarked that the similarity between them was uncanny. But the truth of the matter was that Jack had a front-row seat to every race and every practice session his grandad had ever taken part in, right from the start. He'd even taken his grandad's famous number ten.

Jack had gone back on several occasions. Seeing his grandad race still gave him the best feeling in the world. But this time he wasn't travelling back to watch his grandad race. He'd just become world champion, so there really was only one thing Jack wanted to see.

He stood and watched the celebrations after that final race of 1962. He smiled as his grandad climbed from his car, ran over and hugged his grandma before giving her a passionate kiss on the lips. This time, Jack didn't look away; he savoured the image. Their love had been there from the start.

Jack felt a pang in his chest. He wanted to feel his grandad's arms around him, to smell his old newsboy cap, just one more time. Was that too much to ask?

As his grandparents walked away, arm-in-arm, Jack headed home, ready to deal with everything that came with being a racing world champion.

The following morning Jack woke with a start, panting and covered in sweat. He rubbed his hands over his face, feeling disorientated for a moment. And then he remembered his dream. It had been so vivid, so real ...

... He'd been in the time machine, once again travelling to watch his grandad race. But, when he stepped outside, he was surrounded by crisp, brilliant white as far as the eye could see. No buildings. No vehicles. No animals or people. Nothing but a vast empty void. But then he heard voices. Two of them. Where were they coming from? Jack looked down. White smoke billowed around his ankles and covered his feet.

Two figures appeared and floated towards him. The sight of them made his heart pound faster. They were sitting at a white table, arguing over a game of chess.

'You're nothing but a cheat.'

'No, I'm not! You need to concentrate on the game. You're too nervous. You know he'll be fine.'

'Don't change the subject, we both know you're a cheat. Chess is a game for gentlemen, which is why I'm shocked you play!'

Neither of them had seen Jack. They didn't even know he was there.

Jack finally stepped towards them and both men turned.

'Well?' asked one of them, hurrying to his feet and knocking his chair over. It didn't make a sound as it disappeared into the billowing smoke.

'I did it. I won. I'm World Champion,' beamed Jack, tears prickling his eyes.

It was the first time he'd acknowledged that he was the best driver in the world; like his grandad had been all those years ago. This was all Jack had ever wanted – to emulate his hero, and now that he'd accomplished that, he was overcome with emotion and the tears flowed.

'That's my boy, Jack,' said Herbert, placing his old newsboy cap on his grandson's head and hugging him. 'That's my boy!'

At the table, William Bertrand, wearing his old brown dustcoat and colourful bow tie, watched in silence while blowing plumes of impossible red smoke high into the air ...

... Jack stretched and rolled onto his side. His nostrils filled with a familiar smell. He closed his eyes and took in a lungful of the aroma. It brought back so many happy memories. Memories that would live with him forever.

'I did it, Grandad,' said Jack, pulling the old newsboy cap in tightly to his chest. 'I did it.'

He could almost hear his grandad's smooth, velvet tones. 'That's my boy, Jack. That's my boy.'

Thank Yous

Writing this book has been so much fun, and there are a team of people I wish to thank.

Firstly, I must thank Paul Taylor-McCartney and the whole team at Hermitage Press who saw something special in my writing that made them want to publish *Jack and the Time Machine*.

Secondly, the brilliant and tenacious Sarah Dawes, my editor, who, through her fantastic attention to detail, has made the adventures of Jack and Herbert more exciting and realistic than I could have possibly imagined.

A huge thank you must also be given to Lucy Smith, my illustrator and cover designer, who brought Jack, Herbert and the time machine to life. If I ever design my own time machine, Lucy will be the first person I call.

I must also thank my proof-readers, Wendy Wilkinson, Liz Rapson, Steve Burrows and Jo Murch, who have given valuable advice throughout this whole process.

Finally, the biggest thank you must go to my children: Amy, Lola and Lewis, my three musketeers. Their constant demands for funny stories on long car journeys and at bedtimes, coupled with their laughter and unconditional love, were ultimately responsible for reigniting my love of storytelling.